FOLLOW YOUR HEART

She forced herself to dress in one of her loveliest gowns. In fact it was the prettiest she had bought to wear in London before she was able to come and live in the country.

She had not been invited to a ball or party important enough to wear it so it had languished in her wardrobe and never been seen.

Now as she pulled it on she wished she was going to a glamorous ball in London where she might meet the Prince Charming of her dreams. A man who would love the same things she loved and understand what she felt about life.

'We would both know the moment we met,' she pondered, 'that we were meant for each other.'

She looked at her reflection in the mirror as she dreamed on.

'There would be no need for words as my heart would reach out towards his heart. After that it would only be a question of how soon we told each other of our love.'

But it was just a dream.

THE BARBARA CARTLAND PINK COLLECTION

Titles in this series

FOLLOW YOUR HEART

BARBARA CARTLAND

Barbaracartland.com Ltd

Copyright © 2008 by Cartland Promotions

First published on the internet in June 2008
by Barbaracartland.com

ISBN 978-1-905155-93-4

Printed and bound in Great Britain by Cle-Print Ltd,
St Ives, Cambridgeshire.

THE BARBARA CARTLAND PINK COLLECTION

Barbara Cartland was the most prolific bestselling author in the history of the world. She was frequently in the Guinness Book of Records for writing more books in a year than any other living author. In fact her most amazing literary feat was when her publishers asked for more Barbara Cartland romances, she doubled her output from 10 books a year to over 20 books a year, when she was 77.

She went on writing continuously at this rate for 20 years and wrote her last book at the age of 97, thus completing 400 books between the ages of 77 and 97.

Her publishers finally could not keep up with this phenomenal output, so at her death she left 160 unpublished manuscripts, something again that no other author has ever achieved.

Now the exciting news is that these 160 original unpublished Barbara Cartland books are already being published and by Barbaracartland.com exclusively on the internet, as the international web is the best possible way of reaching so many Barbara Cartland readers around the world.

The 160 books are published monthly and will be numbered in sequence.

The series is called the Pink Collection as a tribute to Barbara Cartland whose favourite colour was pink and it became very much her trademark over the years.

The Barbara Cartland Pink Collection is published only on the internet. Log on to www.barbaracartland.com to find out how you can purchase the books monthly as they are published, and take out a subscription that will ensure that all subsequent editions are delivered to you by mail order to your home.

NEW

Barbaracartland.com is proud to announce the publication of ten new Audio Books for the first time as CDs. They are favourite Barbara Cartland stories read by well-known actors and actresses and each story extends to 4 or 5 CDs. The Audio Books are as follows :

The Patient Bridegroom	The Passion and the Flower
A Challenge of Hearts	Little White Doves of Love
A Train to Love	The Prince and the Pekinese
The Unbroken Dream	A King in Love
The Cruel Count	A Sign of Love

More Audio Books will be published in the future and the above titles can be purchased by logging on to the website www.barbaracartland.com or please write to the address below.

If you do not have access to a computer, you can write for information about the Barbara Cartland Pink Collection and the Barbara Cartland Audio Books to the following address :

Barbara Cartland.com Ltd.
Camfield Place,
Hatfield,
Hertfordshire AL9 6JE
United Kingdom.
Telephone: +44 (0)1707 642629
Fax: +44 (0)1707 663041

THE LATE DAME BARBARA CARTLAND

Barbara Cartland who sadly died in May 2000 at the age of nearly 99 was the world's most famous romantic novelist who wrote 723 books in her lifetime with worldwide sales of over 1 billion copies and her books were translated into 36 different languages.

As well as romantic novels, she wrote historical biographies, 6 autobiographies, theatrical plays, books of advice on life, love, vitamins and cookery. She also found time to be a political speaker and television and radio personality.

She wrote her first book at the age of 21 and this was called *Jigsaw*. It became an immediate bestseller and sold 100,000 copies in hardback and was translated into 6 different languages. She wrote continuously throughout her life, writing bestsellers for an astonishing 76 years. Her books have always been immensely popular in the United States, where in 1976 her current books were at numbers 1 & 2 in the B. Dalton bestsellers list, a feat never achieved before or since by any author.

Barbara Cartland became a legend in her own lifetime and will be best remembered for her wonderful romantic novels, so loved by her millions of readers throughout the world.

Her books will always be treasured for their moral message, her pure and innocent heroines, her good looking and dashing heroes and above all her belief that the power of love is more important than anything else in everyone's life.

"Throughout my entire life I have always followed my heart and I can truthfully say that my heart was right every single time."

Barbara Cartland

CHAPTER ONE
1878

Riding back through he woods, Della was thinking just how lucky she was.

She adored the countryside and the woods in spring held a fascination which was irresistible.

She found there was for her a special magic which seemed more intense than anything that happened in the everyday world outside.

She could not explain it to herself.

As she was an only child she had never had anyone to share her thoughts with.

Her parents, who were now both dead, had been so content with each other and although they adored their daughter, she could not enter into their world of love.

After her father was killed fighting in the Sudan, Della and her mother had kept house for his brother in London. He was Lord Lainden and Secretary of State for Foreign Affairs in the British Government.

He therefore spent a great deal of time abroad and was delighted to have his sister-in-law and her small daughter keep, as he said, his 'house warm'.

A year ago Della's mother had died of pneumonia

during a very cold winter. She had been happy to go, as she wanted to be at peace with her husband.

Della had felt very lonely without her. However, there had already been even more changes during the year.

Her uncle decided it was time for him to retire as he found continually making journeys across the Continent was very exhausting. He had therefore been made a Peer so that he could join the House of Lords, which he attended occasionally, but he was really content to move to the country.

It was where he had always felt he belonged and to Della it was a joy beyond words because she could ride.

As she had inherited the same passion for horses from her father, she had been allowed to ride in Rotten Row, but it was not the same as being able to gallop over the countryside where they were living now.

Lord Lainden had, in fact, been very lucky as he had shared a great friendship whilst he was Secretary of State with the Duke of Marchwood. They had been at the same school together but had drifted apart.

The Duke had come into his title and a certain amount of land in France and he therefore found his old friend very useful.

When Lord Lainden wished to retire the Duke had offered him a house on his estate in Hampshire and with the house went a hundred acres of land.

As the Duke had made the price very low, in fact it was almost a gift, Lord Lainden was extremely grateful.

Della found life in the country was marvellous! The Duke told her uncle that she could help exercise his horses and ride over his estate which extended for several thousand acres.

At just over eighteen Della should have been making her curtsy to Queen Victoria at the Royal Court in Windsor.

She should also be attending the balls and other entertainments arranged for *debutantes* in Society.

She had, however, although her uncle had made the suggestion, refused to go back to London.

"I could easily find you a chaperone, Della," he had persisted. "There are always Society women who are hard-up and are therefore prepared to chaperone *debutantes*.

Della did not speak and he continued,

"They are usually either orphaned as you are or their parents for some reason or another cannot look after them."

"I do want to stay in the country, Uncle Edward," Della had replied. "I have never been so happy as I am now being able to ride all the wonderful horses His Grace keeps in his stables."

She gave a little laugh before adding,

"I can assure you that they are far more amusing than any of the young men who ask me to dance!"

Lord Lainden chuckled as he too wanted to remain in the country with Della.

He was determined for one example to make his garden the most outstanding in the County and there was a stream running through his estate where he could fish for trout.

It was certainly a change after the hurly-burly of diplomacy and the endless travelling which had occupied his life as Secretary of State.

He found it a joy to take life leisurely and not to

have a dozen appointments waiting for him every day.

He also enjoyed the company of his niece as he realised she was exceptionally intelligent. Because they had been in London she had been well educated at one of the fashionable Seminaries for young gentlewomen.

On his clear insistence she had been taught a large number of languages and because he was in politics, Della took a real interest in what was happening both at home and abroad.

She enjoyed all their discussions enormously and actually when Lord Lainden was talking to his niece he often thought he might have been discussing the same subject with a Cabinet Minister.

This morning after breakfast the grooms from the Duke's house – Wood Hall – had brought her three horses.

She was to choose which one she preferred for her morning ride. They were all new stallions in the Duke's stables and the Head Groom was anxious to try them out with a side saddle.

Della had a long conversation with him about the three horses and finally she chose a bay which seemed more spirited than the other two.

"I knows you can 'andle 'im, Miss Della," said the Head Groom. "At the same time I thinks it'd be a mistake for you to jump 'im till you be more acquainted, so to speak."

Della laughed.

"I am sure I shall soon be. But of course you are right, Grayer, and I will not take him over any jumps until you tell me I can do so."

Grayer, who had been with the Duke for many years, smiled at her.

He knew she was an exceptional rider and yet she always had the courtesy to consult him and listen to his opinion. As he had said to his wife,

"Be more than I can say for them stuck-up ladies what comes to the 'all and thinks they knows better than them as lives in the country."

As this was an old grievance his wife had merely laughed. Yet she was well aware that Miss Della had 'a way with her' and this pleased all the servants with whom she came into contact.

Della galloped her chosen stallion which was called Samson until he had settled down to a comfortable trot.

Then as time was moving on she had taken him into the woods. Now he obeyed her by trotting slowly and she could enjoy seeing the small rabbits scuttling ahead on the mossy paths and the red squirrels climbing up the trees.

The birds were singing overhead and she thought the leaves on the trees were swaying gently to the songs they sang.

'How could anything be lovelier?' she asked herself. Then as she was passing through an opening in the wood she saw something unexpected.

It was the top of a gypsy caravan.

It told her that the Romany gypsies, who came to visit them every year, had arrived.

She had to ride a little further on to find a path which led her into the field where they were camped. She had known these particular gypsies for five years as before her uncle had rented the house on the Duke's estate she had often stayed with him and her parents at Wood Hall.

She had always been fascinated by the gypsies. They were so different to other people she knew.

She had always talked to the gypsies and tried to learn to speak their language.

Now she had forgotten that it was time for them to be visiting Hampshire again. Actually it was a little earlier than they usually came.

The Lees, as these particular gypsies were called, were Romanies. They had lived in England for most of their lives and yet they spoke Romani amongst themselves and had never lost their foreign accent.

They had black flashing eyes and very dark hair and were much more cultivated than many of the gypsies Della passed on the roads or those selling their clothes pegs to the cottagers.

When she emerged from the wood into the field there were, as she expected, five caravans.

She thought they looked prettier every time she saw them. They were drawn up almost in a circle and in the centre a fire had been lit on which they would cook rabbit stew or whatever else they were planning for their evening meal.

As Della rode towards them their Chief, Piramus Lee, was waiting for her.

He was a tall man with jet black hair and a fine figure even though he was going on for sixty.

He ruled his family with a rod of iron. Other gypsies who appeared in the neighbourhood and who had no connection with the Lees treated him with respect.

When Della reached him he bowed and greeted her,

"Welcome, Lady. We hoping we'd see you after we arrived yesternight."

"I am delighted you are back," Della told him. "How is everyone? Of course I am longing to hear what adventures you have had since this time last year."

As she was speaking the other gypsies became aware that she was present and they came hurrying out of their caravans.

There was a very pretty girl called Silvaina, who was Piramus's granddaughter. She was about the same age as Della and she ran eagerly up to her saying,

"It's fine to see you, Lady. We was talkin' of you when us was comin' here and hoping you'd visit us."

"Of course I would visit you as soon as I knew you had arrived," replied Della. "As I was riding in the woods I saw your caravans. How are you all?"

By this time there was quite a crowd assembling.

There was Piramus's son Luke and his nephew called Abram. They were two years older than Silvaina and as they talked, their mothers and fathers emerged from their caravans.

They came towards Della slowly and when she thought they were all present, she looked round and asked,

"Where is Lendi?"

She was the oldest member of the family, the mother of Piramus, and noted for being a very famous fortune-teller.

Piramus shook his head.

"Mother not well," he exclaimed. "She cannot leave caravan. I sure she be very honoured if Lady visit her."

"Of course I will visit her."

Della asked Abram to hold her horse and slipped to the ground.

"I am so sorry your mother is not well," she said to Piramus. "The villagers will be terribly upset if she is not able to tell their fortunes."

"Able to do one or two," answered Piramus. "Mireli take lessons from her. In time she be very good fortune-teller."

"That is marvellous news. Everyone wants to know the future and who could predict it better than a Romany?"

"Who indeed?" Piramus replied with a note of satisfaction.

They reached the beautifully decorated caravan which Della remembered belonged to Lendi.

She climbed up the steps and as the door was open she bent her head to enter the caravan.

Lendi was lying in a bed propped up with pillows. Her white hair made the darkness of her eyes look even more mysterious than ever. When she saw Della she put out her hand.

"Lady, come see me!" she cried. "That kind."

"I am upset to hear that you have to stay in bed, dear Lendi. What are we all going to do if you cannot tell us about the future?"

Lendi gave a laugh.

"I tell your future, Lady, no need cards."

"What is my future?"

"You find – happiness."

Lendi closed her eyes for a moment and then she spoke in a voice which she always used when she was predicting.

"Lady find – what she seek – but she go search for it. When Lady – find surprise."

She spoke the words very slowly and reaching out her hand covered Della's.

"The moon protect you," she continued. "You be afraid – no reason. You have – magic which cannot be – take away."

Her hand on Della's was very cold.

When she opened her eyes there was a glint in them which told Della there was still life in her body and she was certain that Lendi would not die yet.

"Thank you" she said aloud. "I ought to cross your palm with silver, but I have no money with me.

The old gypsy cackled.

"No money necessary 'tween friends. You, Lady befriend us. We do anything – help you."

"I know," said Della quietly, "and I am very grateful. But you must take care of yourself, Lendi, because the family of Lee would not be the same without you."

"When my time come, Lady, they manage. The powers I have – pass to another of family."

"I hear that is to be Mireli."

Lendi nodded her head.

"That true. The power is there within her. One day she take my place."

"That is such good news, but at the same time, Lendi, as you know we all love you. It will be very difficult for anyone to take your place in our hearts."

She knew by the smile the old woman gave her that she was pleased with the compliment.

As she had been talking to her Della had been kneeling by her bedside and now she bent forward and kissed Lendi's cheek.

"I will come again tomorrow," she promised, "and

bring you flowers from our garden and strawberries which are just beginning to ripen."

"Very kind Lady – kindness is rewarded!"

"If there is anything else you want you must tell me," Della told her as she moved towards the door. "I expect by now the village will have learned you are here and they will be coming to ask for your help and guidance which you have always given them."

"Mireli do that – now."

Della climbed down the steps of the caravan.

The gypsy horses had all been taken away and with their back legs tethered they were cropping the grass outside the ring of caravans.

Most of the other members of the family were waiting for her.

"My mother very pleased see Lady," piped up Piramus.

"She was telling me that Mireli is to take her place, but no one can do that. She is an institution and I have a feeling that the villagers will not believe anyone else as they have always believed her."

"Mireli has gift," replied Piramus. "The stars teach her. Family never end."

Della knew that he was making it clear there was always continuity in the family and she was sure it would never be broken. As she thought about it she remembered hearing that Lendi had taken the place of her own mother, who had also been a famous fortune-teller in her time.

As if he could read her thoughts, Piramus said,

"Line never broken. For all Lees when life done – another fill empty place."

"You are *so* wise," exclaimed Della. "But I hope

that Lendi will not leave us for a long time yet."

Piramus made a gesture with his hands, which told her that he was saying, without words, that it was in the lap of the Gods.

Della shook hands with two of the gypsies she had not spoken to before and then she walked to her horse with Piramus beside her.

"You must tell me if there is anything you need, Piramus. My uncle will be only too pleased to provide you with eggs from our hens and any vegetables you want from the garden."

"Lady very generous. We kneel at feet."

Piramus helped Della onto the saddle and she thanked Abram for looking after her horse.

"I will come back to see you tomorrow," she called as she rode away.

The gypsies waved until she re-entered the wood. She rode home thinking that her uncle would be interested in knowing the Lees were with them again and he would doubtless go and speak to them himself.

When she reached the entrance to their drive she saw that the gate was open and wondered if anyone was calling on her uncle. She hoped it would not be with a problem which would take him back to London.

Twice last month the Prime Minister had sent for him and he had felt obliged to journey back to Downing Street.

'If Mr. Disraeli is bothering him again,' Della said to herself, 'I shall be very angry. After all he is retired and Lord Derby, who has taken his place, should be able to manage.'

She realised, however, it was really a great

compliment. It was not only the Prime Minister who asked her uncle's advice as when problems arose there were those in other positions who also asked for his help.

After making a turn in the drive Della could see there was an impressive carriage outside the front door and even though it was still some distance from her she knew who it belonged to.

This knowledge took away her anxiety about her uncle.

The visitor was not someone from London, but the Duke himself from Wood Hall.

He had been away last week and she now remembered he had been expected back either yesterday or the day before. In fact her uncle had awaited a message from the Hall to say that the Duke wanted to see him.

It was not surprising that the Duke turned to his greatest friend for company as his wife was a semi-invalid and seldom left the house. His son lived in France and his two daughters were married.

Although there were parties from time to time at Wood Hall, Della was aware that the Duke was often lonely.

He did not possess the brains of her uncle, but he was still an intelligent man. He liked talking seriously as well as being amusing.

It was not surprising that more than anyone else he sought the company of his oldest friend.

There were, of course, many relations and one or two of them were invariably staying at the Hall. Della had found most of them rather dull.

She suspected the Duke felt the same and as she rode on up the drive she thought,

'As he is here, I expect he will stay for luncheon so I must warn cook.'

Mrs. Beston had been with her uncle for a large number of years. She was always ready at a moment's notice to provide His Grace with the food he particularly liked.

He had a number of favourite dishes which, fortunately, did not take long to prepare.

As she was getting on in years, Mrs. Beston did not like to be hurried.

'I must find out if he is staying for luncheon as quickly as possible,' Della told herself.

She hurried Samson forward and took him directly into the stables.

"How did you get on, Miss Della?" Grayer asked as he took hold of Samson's bridle.

"He went like the wind and behaved like a Saint! We will have no trouble with him."

"Not while you're a-ridin' 'im, miss. The stable boys were a-findin' 'im a bit of an 'andful."

Della smiled.

"He will settle down."

She then hurried over the cobble-stones and into the house by the kitchen door to find Mrs. Beston.

The kitchen boasted old-fashioned beams across the ceiling from which were hanging ducks and chickens, sides of bacon and onions.

"Good Morning, Mrs. Beston," Della called as she entered. "I expect you know that His Grace is here and as it is a quarter-to-one, I am certain he will stay for luncheon."

"That's just what I guessed too, miss. I says to Mr. Storton as I've said a hundred times afore, why can't I be given notice of when His Grace be a-coming so I has them dishes he likes ready for him?"

Della had heard this grumble many times and she merely smiled.

"However difficult it may be, Mrs. Beston, I am sure you will not fail His Grace."

She did not answer. She merely snorted and turned round to stir a sauce which was simmering on top of the fire.

Della left the kitchen and ran along the corridor which led into the hall. She saw Storton the butler standing there with a footman. The boy had only been taken on recently and was being taught his job.

"I suppose His Grace is staying for luncheon," Della enquired as she went towards the stairs.

"We haven't been told nothing yet, Miss Della," replied Storton.

Della hurried to her room knowing that her uncle would not like her to sit down to luncheon in her riding habit even though she might be riding again in the afternoon.

She changed into a pretty cotton dress and quickly tidied her hair, whilst her maid buttoned up the back of her gown.

"Hurry, Emily, or I will be late."

"We've two minutes, miss, and his Lordship'll take that to walk from the study."

Della giggled.

"Whatever happens Uncle Edward will enter the dining room on the stroke of one o'clock. He has always said he owes his success to being punctual while other people are always late."

The maid did not answer and Della thought she did not really understand. It was after all an old family joke. Because Lord Lainden was invariably precisely on time he had often managed to gain an advantage over his political opponents.

As Della ran down the stairs, the grandfather clock in the hall struck the hour.

As it did so, her uncle was walking along the passage which led to his study.

He was accompanied by the Duke.

Reaching the bottom of the stairs, Della ran towards them.

"I am back, Uncle Edward," she puffed, "and exactly on time."

She curtsied to the Duke, who bent and kissed her cheek.

"How are you, my dear, or is that a silly question?" he asked. "You look very pretty and there is a flush in your cheeks which tells me you have been riding again."

"Yes, indeed I have and it is one of your horses which I highly recommend as being outstanding even amongst the rest of your stable."

"That is most interesting, my dear, and I must certainly try the newcomer for myself. What is his name?"

"Most appropriately – Samson, and as I always imagine the great man to have been not only strong but intelligent and with an irresistible charm, that accolade also applies to your stallion!"

The Duke chortled.

"What a very excellent recommendation and one I hope you will soon be applying to a man."

As he finished speaking he moved towards the front door and to her surprise Della realised he was leaving.

"Why are you not staying for luncheon?" she asked.

The Duke shook his head.

"I have a number of people waiting for me at the Hall and fortunately luncheon is at one-thirty as my sister is arriving from London, so I will not be late."

He looked at Lord Lainden as he spoke and his eyes twinkled in case he might be accused of the crime of being late.

Then as the Duke took his hat from the footman he turned to say,

"Goodbye, Edward, and I shall be waiting eagerly to hear your answer to my question."

Lord Lainden did not reply. He walked to the door to watch the Duke hurry into the waiting carriage.

The footman, wearing an impressive uniform, closed the carriage door before climbing up onto the box beside the coachman.

As the horses moved off, the Duke bent forward to raise his hand and Lord Lainden waved back.

The carriage proceeded swiftly down the drive.

"I felt sure he would stay to luncheon," sighed Della.

"He has rather important friends staying with him," commented her uncle, "and now we must not keep *our* luncheon waiting."

He walked quickly towards the dining room with Della following him.

She wondered vaguely what the answer might be to the Duke's important question, but her uncle spoke of other matters as soon as they sat down.

She thought it must be something confidential which could not be discussed in front of the servants.

The luncheon was excellent, but Della thought Mrs. Beston would be disappointed that the Duke had not stayed.

She had, however, a great deal to tell her uncle about her ride and that the gypsies were now in residence in the field beside Long Wood where they camped year after year.

"So they are back!" exclaimed Lord Lainden. "That is good and of course I must go and see them."

"They will be very disappointed if you do not."

Della then told him how Lendi was now bedridden and added that Mireli was learning to take her place.

She knew her uncle was listening intently, but at the same time she had the feeling there was something on his mind.

And it was worrying him.

Because her mother had been of Scottish descent, Della had often thought she was fey and even as a child she was aware of secrets happening around her, events which would never have occurred to other children of the same age.

When she grew older she found she knew things which grown-ups either kept hidden or were not aware of themselves.

Sometimes she found herself predicting an occurrence before it happened.

When she had first stayed at Wood Hall she had

been aware of the ghost before anyone else told her about it.

'I wonder what is worrying Uncle Edward,' she pondered before luncheon was over.

She knew her uncle so well. He never had to tell her when he was faced with a difficult political problem as she was aware of it from the way he spoke or perhaps it came from his vibrations.

She was glad it was the Duke who had been the visitor as otherwise she would have been suspicious that he was being asked once again to go abroad. Perhaps it would be either to Paris, Berlin or Amsterdam to settle some international difficulty for which no one else could find a solution.

But it was the Duke who had brought a note of discord to the house.

Della therefore supposed it must be something to do with his family. At one time there had been a monumental crisis when the Duke's nephew became infatuated with a most unsuitable woman. If it had just been an *affaire-de-coeur* no one would have worried particularly.

The gossips would soon have found someone else to talk about, but the Duke, however, had learned that his nephew was contemplating marrying the woman in question.

She was absolutely determined to make herself a Duchess and the Duke had, of course, turned to Lord Lainden in despair. It was not surprising to Della that her uncle with his usual brilliance and understanding of people had in some way managed to get rid of the woman and at least there had been no scandal.

She wondered now if it was one of the Duke's family who was in trouble again or alternatively it might be just something wrong on the estate.

Whatever it was she realised that it was worrying her uncle.

She considered that it was rather tiresome of the Duke not to try to solve his own problems.

It was so important for her Uncle Edward to rest.

He was, in fact, writing his memoirs which Della found extremely interesting. He had known so many famous politicians and had travelled to so many fascinating countries. In addition he possessed a sardonic sense of humour that was all his own.

She was certain that his book, when it was finished, would be a best-seller. The difficulty with her uncle, however, was that he always wanted everything done immediately on time and at a moment's notice!

That was quite impossible where a book was concerned as there was so much he had to look up and so much he had to remember.

Della longed to help him and yet it was impossible for her to do more than encourage and praise him. She was also able to point out any passage she found difficult to understand.

Luncheon was not a large meal. Lord Lainden was usually in a hurry at midday, but was prepared to relax in the evening.

As the coffee was served Della asked,

"What are you going to do this afternoon, Uncle Edward?"

"I think after what you have told me, I will ride down and see the Lees at the gypsy camp, but first I want to talk to you, so let us go into the study."

Now, Della thought, she would hear what had been

worrying him.

Equally there was a serious note in his voice which made her think it was a somewhat serious problem. She wished the Duke would not come to upset them and it was particularly annoying when her uncle had been in such a good mood for the last two or three days.

He had just completed a whole chapter of his book and Della had expected him to continue writing this afternoon so that they could discuss what he had done at dinner time.

Yet he suddenly wanted to go riding and visit the Lees, almost before they had settled down. This was something he had never done before and she could not help thinking that whatever the Duke had said was really worrying him.

As they walked down the corridor Lord Lainden put his hand on Della's shoulder.

"You know how much I love having you here with me, my dear," he began. 'In fact you have brought sunshine into the house which has made a great deal of difference to me and to everyone else."

Della looked at him in surprise.

"That is a very sweet compliment to pay me, Uncle Edward, but I cannot help wondering why you have done so now."

They had reached the study door and her uncle took his hand from her shoulder.

"That is just what I am going to tell you, my dear Della."

They walked into the room.

As Della expected her uncle went to stand in front of the fireplace as he invariably did when he was discussing anything important. In the winter the fire was warming, but now the fireplace was merely filled with plants, which created a patch of colour while looking very attractive.

Della sat down in one of the armchairs in front of her uncle.

She thought as she looked at him that despite his age he was a very good-looking and attractive man. There was an air of authority and gravitas about him which was to be expected after his distinguished career.

Although his hair was turning white, it still covered his head and he was by no means bald.

Silhouetted against a magnificent picture of horses by Stubbs, he looked, she decided, exactly as an Englishman should and it would be difficult even at his age to find anyone to rival him.

Although she had sat down, Lord Lainden had not spoken.

"What is worrying you, Uncle Edward?" asked Della quietly. "I cannot think why His Grace must bring all his problems to you."

Lord Lainden smiled.

"He expects me to solve them for him, my dear, as you are well aware. But this one actually concerns *you*."

Della looked astonished.

"Concerns me! – but why *me*? – and about what?"

There was a pause before Lord Lainden replied simply,

"Jason has come home."

CHAPTER TWO

Della stared at the uncle in sheer astonishment.

"Jason has come home!" she exclaimed. "I do *not* believe it."

"It is true and I thought you would be surprised."

"I am astonished. But why after all these years?"

They were speaking about the Duke's only son, the Earl of Rannock, who had lived abroad in France for the last five years.

He had always been a raffish young man.

When he grew older, although his father and everyone else begged him to settle down, he refused. He spent his time with the fastest and most questionable Society beauties when he was living in London.

Then he journeyed to Paris and the stories of the parties he gave and the women he gave them for were the talk of his relatives and friends. The gossips of Mayfair naturally found him an irresistible subject of their conversation.

Perhaps only Lord Lainden knew how deeply hurt the Duke was by the behaviour of his son and heir.

He certainly tried in every possible way to make Jason see sense and behave more reasonably.

Of course he suggested he should marry and have a family.

If Jason did not do so, the title and the estate would pass to an obscure cousin on the Duke's death and he was unmarried and nearly as old as the Duke.

It seemed as if the Dukedom might be lost forever and there would be no future Earl of Rannock. The Dukedom was extremely old and could be traced back to the Battle of Agincourt.

To say that the Duke was proud of his antecedence was to put it mildly. To him it was almost sacred.

He had spent a lifetime improving Wood Hall and the estate and he had collected every possible portrait he could find of his many ancestors.

The Duke had many relatives, but there were none in the direct line except for Jason.

Jason had been in trouble ever since he was born.

He was a sour sickly child who became almost uncontrollable as he grew stronger. He behaved so badly when he was sent to Eton that the Headmaster threatened to expel him.

It was understandable that when Jason appeared in the Social world, women pursued him for his title and his money.

However, he chose the most outrageous and notorious females to be his closest associates and in vain the Duke begged his more respectable friends to invite Jason to their parties, but he refused them all.

Otherwise he behaved so badly when he did attend they never asked him again.

In some ways it was a relief when he moved out of England announcing that he found London boring and bought a house in Paris.

It was impossible for people not to learn how he was behaving in France and for the Duke not to hear about it.

Over and over again, as Della knew, the Duke had rushed to her uncle with a story of Jason's latest outrageous behaviour. At times he seemed almost in tears.

That Jason ran up enormous bills was immaterial as what the Duke wanted was for him to marry some suitable young lady and then he could take over the running of the estate.

Jason's answer was very clear.

He was not interested in country life or country pursuits.

He rode and he drove in the Bois de Boulogne in Paris accompanied by the most fantastic Parisian *cocottes*, who he encouraged to be even more outlandish than he was.

Della was a schoolgirl when her parents were living in London and the Duke's relatives would whisper about Jason when she was present. Yet invariably sooner or later, she heard of his latest escapade.

Now she remembered that three years ago when she was only fifteen, the balloon had gone up.

Jason had married without informing his father until after the ceremony had taken place and when the Duke had heard the news, he nearly died of shock.

He learnt that Jason had married one of the most notorious of all the *cocottes* in Paris. She had already been the mistress of two Princes and the King of the Netherlands!

When Lord Lainden was first informed he was immediately suspicious.

Later he was proved right that the woman had more or less tricked Jason into marriage, craving for his title and his fortune.

But there was no doubt that he was infatuated with her.

He still had, however, as the Duke believed, the decency not to besmirch the family name, so how could Jason marry a woman who they would be ashamed to put on the family tree?

The Duke wanted to find excuses for his son, but it was impossible to escape the anger and the disapproval of his relatives, besides the humiliating pity of his friends.

"There is nothing I can do," he wailed to Lord Lainden in a broken-hearted voice.

"Nothing," was the reply, "except to make sure that Jason stays away from London and perhaps in time this will all be forgotten."

"To think a woman like that will one day be the Chatelaine of Wood Hall makes me wish I was dead," fumed the Duke.

There were no words with which Lord Lainden could comfort him.

Wood Hall had been in the family for five centuries and each generation had made many alterations and improvements. Now it was one of the most famous ancestral homes in England and its collection of pictures, furniture and silver was spoken of with awe.

The woman who Jason had married would reign there in state.

Worse still her children, if she produced any, would be an unthinkable insult to the Marchwood name.

All these recollections flashed though Della's mind

before she asked,

"Why has Jason returned, Uncle Edward?"

"His wife has very conveniently died," he replied, "and he has apologised to his father for his appalling behaviour."

"Apologised!" exclaimed Della.

"I think the truth is that he has passed through a special hell since he married her and it is a great relief to him to be free."

"Well, I suppose it is one step in the right direction, but I should imagine it is doubtful that his repentance is genuine."

She spoke rather sarcastically because she had never liked Jason.

Of course he was very much older than her, but even as a child she considered him an unpleasant man.

He was not good-looking like his father and the last time she had seen him she noted that the debauchery of his life had left its mark on his face.

He had certainly extended the sowing of his 'wild oats' for a long time and now she imagined, as the years had passed, he would look even worse.

She felt extremely sorry for the Duke.

Aloud she said,

"There is nothing you can do, Uncle Edward, so do not upset yourself over Jason, he is not worth it."

There was silence for a moment before Lord Lainden resumed,

"The Duke has come to me with what he feels would be an excellent solution to his problem."

"I cannot imagine what that can possibly be,"

commented Della. "Although his wife is now dead, I expect he will still find another one who is unlikely to be any better than the last."

"The Duke now tells me that he is quite certain Jason is telling the truth when he says he was tricked into marriage. He has now informed his father that he wants to marry sensibly and settle down at the Hall."

"If the Duke believes that, "answered Della, "he must be a great optimist."

"He wants to believe him and he asks for our help to ensure that Jason keeps his word. If he genuinely makes a new life for himself, it will be very different to the way he has lived in the past."

"I would not bet on it," said Della scathingly. "And quite frankly, Uncle Edward, I resent you being worried and upset by Jason."

Her voice became scornful as she continued,

"He has behaved abominably as you well know, made his father and mother miserable and reduced a great number of his relatives to tears."

She had a feeling her uncle was not listening, but carried on insistently,

"One of them told me when we were last in London how ashamed she was that Jason was her cousin. In fact she often thought that people looked at her in a criticising manner in case she in any way should resemble him."

"I can understand that, but the Duke is absolutely convinced that Jason has now seen the error of his ways and of course he wants so much to believe his son."

"He will be lucky if anyone else does," remarked Della.

Her uncle gave her a sharp look as if he resented the

way she was speaking and then he said slowly,

"It is always a mistake not to help those who need our help. The Duke has a suggestion to make which I think we must both consider very seriously."

"What is it?"

"He has said – that it would give him the greatest pleasure and inexplicable happiness *if you married Jason*."

As Lord Lainden finished speaking there was complete and absolute silence.

Della stared at him incredulously.

"*Marry* – Jason!" she managed to exclaim at last. "You cannot be serious. After all he is old enough to be my father!"

"Jason will be thirty-eight in a month's time and if, as his father believes, he is truly penitent of his past behaviour, the one thing that could help him more than anything else would be a sensible and at the same time intelligent wife."

Della did not speak.

After a moment he continued,

"The Duke has always loved you and he has just said that nothing would give him greater pleasure than if you became his daughter-in-law."

"You cannot really – believe I could – accept such a – suggestion?" Della managed to stammer.

Her voice sounded strange even to herself.

"I have not seen Jason for many years," she went on, "but I always disliked him. From what I have heard about him – he is utterly despicable and the last man in the world – I would ever think of marrying."

Her voice seemed to ring out jerkily.

Because she felt so agitated she rose to her feet and walked across the room to the window, where she stood looking out at the garden, but she was not seeing the beauty of the flowers or the blossom on the trees.

She was seeing Jason's debauched face.

She remembered that she had once slipped away from him to hide in her bedroom. It was not that he had made any advances to her or even taken any notice of her because she was only a child.

It was because she was so conscious that he was wicked and she had no wish to come into contact with him.

Now with her back to the room, she blurted out in a different voice,

"I am sorry, Uncle Edward, but you must make it absolutely clear to the Duke – that whoever Jason marries – it will not be *me*!"

There was a long silence until her uncle responded,

"It is not quite as easy as that."

Della turned round.

"What do you mean?"

"I mean, my dear, that the Duke has set his heart on this solution to his problem. He made it very clear to me that he is relying on our friendship for us to assist him or in his own words, 'to save the Marchwood family'."

"That is all very well," stormed Della, "the Duke may be your friend – but he is not our relation. You can, of course, assist him if it is possible to find a woman who would tolerate Jason – but it will not be *me*!"

Again there was silence and she saw the worry on her uncle's face.

"You must not take it so seriously, Uncle Edward. You are sorry for the Duke and so am I, but Jason is his son – not *yours*."

"I know exactly what you are saying, Della, but the Duke made it quite clear what he required and however strange it may seem, he is expecting co-operation both from you and me. As he carefully pointed out we have accepted a great deal from him over the years."

Della was astonished.

"What do you mean, Uncle Edward?"

"I obtained this house so cheaply that it was in fact almost a present from a friend. You have ridden his horses daily and we have been accepted on his estate as if we were part of his family."

He paused for a moment.

"You are allowed to go in and out of the Hall as you please and His Grace's servants will take orders from you as if, as he pointed out, you were actually his daughter."

"I do not believe he could have said all that!" exclaimed Della.

"He said all that and a great deal more. He made it quite clear that if you and I did not help him in this, the most important moment of his life, he had no wish to see either of us again!"

Della sank down into the nearest chair.

She was thinking that if anyone else but her uncle had said this to her, she would not believe them. But he was a gentleman who always spoke the truth, which was why he was always so respected.

Della recognised only too well what it would mean if all the comforts they obtained from the Marchwood estate were to be taken away from them.

It was not only that she could enjoy the freedom of the horses, the fields and the woods, but the Duke's Home Farm supplied them regularly with butter, milk, cream, chickens, eggs and ducks.

There was always lamb for luncheon if they wanted it and the bacon was home-cured.

When she thought it over there were a hundred advantages which came from Wood Hall and like her uncle she had always accepted them gratefully.

At the same time they had been inclined to look on it almost as if it was theirs by right.

Della had always known that the Duke could be a hard task-master if he was opposed by any of his staff and yet because he had always appeared to love her uncle and herself, she had never seen that side of him.

Now he was determined to have his own way and she could understand why he wanted her to marry his prodigal son.

He knew her so well and, as her uncle had said, loved her.

She was aware that any woman Jason married would have to be strong-minded enough to make him keep to his promise of penitence.

Who else with these qualities was it possible for the Duke to find quickly?

'I will not do it,' Della told herself, but equally she was very conscious that her uncle was frightened of the future.

He was not a rich man now he had retired, but he was what might be called 'comfortably off'. He did not have to spend much money on living and he certainly did not crave for the expensive life which he would have had to live in London.

In fact, he was happy here in the country – very happy.

Yet so much of his happiness depended on the Duke.

'What can I do? What *can* I do?' Della asked herself.

Her uncle was looking at her and after a moment he said,

"I have, of course, told Ralph that it was impossible for me to make up your mind for you and that Jason must do his own wooing."

"You mean he is here?"

"He is at present in London buying himself some new clothes and as I understand trying to conciliate some of the family who he has not been in contact with for years."

"And he is coming to Wood Hall?"

"In three days time when his father will send him here to meet you or if you would prefer we can go to the Hall."

Della wanted to say that she would do neither, but she recognised it would be banging her head against a brick wall.

She was perceptive enough to realise that her uncle was convinced it would be to her advantage, as well as the Duke's if she married Jason.

She knew at the back of his mind he would love her to become a Duchess and she would have control of Wood Hall with all its treasures and naturally the Marchwood jewels were legendary.

She could read his mind – he was thinking of the Duke's enormous stables with the magnificent horses she enjoyed riding.

Surely her uncle was not thinking that all these riches would be some compensation for losing her childish dreams of marrying the man she had fallen in love with?

'If it is a childish dream,' mused Della, 'it is still deep in my heart.'

She had always believed that one day she would ride in the woods with the man she loved.

He would love her and understand the stories she told herself. He would believe, as she did, that the goblins worked underground and the nymphs lived in the pool. Under the trees the fairies danced at night and left a mushroom circle on the grass.

All her fantasies would mean as much to him as they did to her and become an intrinsic part of their love.

She had known how much her father and mother meant to each other and she believed that one day it was the love she would find. A love that would make any setbacks bearable however difficult because they were together.

They would always be happy and content and whether they were living in a Palace or a cave they would both be facing the world together.

How could Wood Hall with all its treasures compensate for having to be touched by a man she despised?

A man who had made himself notorious with the lowest women to be found in both London and Paris.

'I – cannot do it – *I cannot*!' Della told herself.

She knew her uncle was waiting for her to speak, not impatiently but somehow despairingly.

Once again she rose from her chair and walked to

the window.

"I am afraid, my dear, this will come as a shock to you," he said, "but of course nothing will be decided too quickly. But the Duke is afraid that Jason might change his mind and if he is bored here, he will return to France."

"Does he really believe that Jason is penitent enough," demanded Della, "to spend the rest of his life – in the country? It has never amused him in the past. Will he be content with one woman rather than the dozens he has been associating with?"

"The Duke wants to believe that Jason is being honest when he says he has finished with his past life. His unhappy marriage has made him realise he has been a fool and, as I have already said, he wants to settle down and have a family."

Della shivered, feeling as if an icy hand had squeezed her heart.

"I, personally," she told her uncle, "think that Jason will soon be bored with the life that we enjoy here. Then what will happen to his wife, whoever she may be?"

"She will perhaps have children to compensate for her husband, but I think, my dear, you are looking too far ahead. What we are concerned with at the moment is that Jason is really sorry for the trouble he has caused and the unhappiness he has brought his parents."

He paused and with difficult Della prevented herself from saying anything further.

"He has agreed," he continued, "that he has associated with the wrong women and, in fact, after his three years of marriage he has no wish to see any of them again."

"Can a leopard really change his spots?" queried

Della mischievously.

"We can only hope and pray that if you do marry Jason," he answered, "you will be clever enough to make him keep his vows and behave as someone in his position should."

"Which he has never done in the past!"

"That is indeed true, but the Duke is absolutely convinced that at present he is very contrite and is longing in every way to make amends for his dissolute behaviour."

He drew in his breath before he added,

"It would be unchristian, unfriendly and certainly unneighbourly to a man who has always been extremely kind to us to refuse our help in what is undoubtedly an acute emergency."

Della turned round and walked back towards her uncle.

"You say that Jason is coming home in three days time? I make no promises, Uncle Edward, but we will arrange a dinner party here and invite the Duke and Jason."

She knew by the expression on her uncle's face how relieved he was by her words.

"I will tell the Duke what you have suggested," he said, "and I know how grateful he will be."

"Please make it clear," Della insisted quickly, "that I am not committed in any way and am just prepared to meet Jason who I have not seen for many years."

"Yes. Yes, of course," he replied rather testily. "That is understood. And there is always a chance that Jason will not wish to marry you."

"Of course."

She spoke almost confidently to please her uncle,

but she was, however, well aware that the Duke was pushing his son with all his strength towards her.

Doubtless from the monetary point of view it made the marriage seem very desirable to Jason. She was quite sure without being told, that he had come home with a multitude of debts as he had always done in the past.

The Duke was a rich man and yet Della had often heard him saying to her uncle that if Jason carried on his usual way, he would undoubtedly become a bankrupt.

For years, because the Duke did not want more scandal than there was already, he had paid up all of his son's debts. He had also increased, year after year, the very large allowance he gave him.

Now, somewhat cynically, Della considered that one of the reasons Jason had returned home was because he had run out of money.

Her uncle was looking at her in an apologetic manner and she sensed that he was ashamed of the sacrifice he was asking her to make.

She walked towards him and kissed his cheek.

"Do not worry, Uncle Edward, perhaps things will not be as bad as we expect. Perhaps the clouds will roll away and carry Jason with them!"

Her uncle laughed as if he could not help it.

"You are being very brave, my dearest, and I admire and respect you for it. I know this is asking a great deal of any girl of your age."

He sighed and continued,

"But then your brain has always been very much older than your body and I know that it makes you understand the predicament we are both in."

"I do understand, Uncle Edward, and I will certainly

think about what can be done, but for the moment – it is very – difficult to see the stars."

She did not wait for her uncle's reply, but walked out of the room.

When she had gone he raised up his hand to wipe his forehead.

He felt he had sweated from a battle which had actually not been as violent or as difficult as he had anticipated.

He was well aware he was committing what was tantamount to a crime.

He was asking a girl who was lovely, pure and innocent to tie herself up in matrimony to a man of Jason's reputation.

His first impulse, when the Duke had spoken to him, was to tell him such an idea was impossible.

Then he soon became aware that his old friend was resolved with an iron determination to get his own way.

He clearly thought that Lord Lainden was about to refuse his suggestion, so without further discussion he began to use every possible threat. In fact short of coming into the open he made it almost a fight to the death.

To the Duke it was a miracle to have his son apologising for his behaviour and promising in every way to conduct himself very differently in the future.

The Duke was obviously conscious that the odds were against him, so he was forced to use every available weapon to ensure that Jason made a new life for himself.

No one would ever know how he and his Duchess had suffered. How they cringed when they continually heard the appalling tales of Jason's debauched behaviour in Paris.

The Duke regularly received astronomical bills he was forced to honour, but it was the humiliation that he found most unbearable, especially when he looked to the future.

How could any man not want to keep and cherish anything as magnificent as Wood Hall not only a treasure belonging to his family but also to the nation? Worse perhaps than anything else the Duke suffered was being pitied by his contemporaries. They knew he was worrying about his son, but they never mentioned him – they just commiserated with him without actually mentioning Jason's name.

'Whatever can I do about Jason?' the Duke had asked himself a thousand times and never found an answer.

Yet now when he least expected it, Jason had returned home.

He had apologised in a way which made his father believe that he was being truthful and honest. He had even offered to make amends.

It was he who had suggested he should make a marriage which his father and mother would approve and he would produce an heir which was so necessary for the future of the Dukedom.

"Find me a wife, Papa," Jason had said. "And then we will be able to forget the past and look forward to a happy future."

It was when the Duke thought he could not be hearing right that Della had sprung into his mind.

He had been watching her riding through the Park only the previous day before he had left for London.

The Park deer were moving out of the way of her

horse and although he was not close to her, he knew how lovely she would be looking.

The curls of her fair hair would be dancing against her white skin with her eyes shining excitedly because she was riding one of his finest and most spirited horses.

The Duke had watched her on many occasions and he had often thought that she looked more like a Goddess than a human being.

She rode, as his Chief Groom continually told him, better than any woman he had ever known.

It was then that the Duke had suddenly awoken to reality.

He realised that Della, with her sportsmanship and her brain, was the only person who could save Jason.

She would be strong-minded enough to force him to keep his promises.

She would be lovely enough to attract him perhaps as no other woman had attracted him in his life.

She would definitely produce children who would make the whole family proud.

'Della! She is the answer!' the Duke had exclaimed to himself and at once he rang a bell to tell a servant he wanted a carriage to take him to Lord Lainden's house.

*

When Della left her uncle she walked out into the garden.

She was beginning to feel that even the roof over her head was confining.

In just the short time she had spent with her uncle he had managed to shatter not only her happiness but her whole feeling of security, something she had always felt with him since her father and mother died.

She has been so happy when they were together.

Actually she had often thought it was quite unnecessary to have many friends as she had never met a young man who was as clever or amusing as her uncle.

No one else made everything they talked about seem so interesting that it was like reading a book she could not put down.

She had also loved every minute since they had come to live in the country. It was impossible for her to put into words her joy of riding the Duke's horses.

It passed through her mind that in the future they would belong to her.

But the thought was immediately followed by a vision of Jason as she had last seen him.

Even to think of him made her shudder.

'How can I possibly be married to a man I loathe and detest?' she asked herself. 'A man who, I do not believe for a moment, is really genuine in what he is now telling his father. A man who has already proved himself a hundred times over to be a liar and a modern Casanova.'

She became uncontrollably agitated.

Instinctively, without realising what she was doing, she was walking across the Park.

It was over a mile and yet it seemed to her, because she was so deep in her thoughts, as if she had just walked out of the front door.

The next moment the Duke's stables were in front of her. There was no one about and so she walked into the first building. The horses were all in their stalls.

The Duke had spent a great deal of money making them comfortable. The stalls were larger than they had been in the past, made to exactly the right height with each horse's name painted on a board above its manger.

Della strolled from stall to stall.

The horses she had ridden nuzzled against her. Her father had taught her many years ago that she must talk to a horse before she rode him to make the animal used to her voice.

And in some strange way this bonding made their personalities join together. It became exactly as if the horse was a human being.

Della thought that as she was fey she almost knew what a horse was thinking. Just as she could read the thoughts of any man or woman.

She had visited about half-a-dozen stalls when Grayer appeared.

"I didn't know you were 'ere, Miss Della. Are you wantin' a ride?"

"That is just what I would love to do at the moment, Grayer, and I will ride just as I am."

She was wearing a thin gown suitable for the warm weather. She wore no hat because she had meant to stay in the garden.

The Head Groom, however, made no comment as he was used to Della riding a horse whenever she wanted.

It took him only a few minutes to put on a side-saddle and then he led Samson out into the yard.

Thanking Grayer she rode off moving instinctively towards the nearest wood.

She felt that only there amongst the fairies, the nymphs, the squirrels and the birds would she be able to think clearly.

When she reached the wood she knew at once why

she had come.

She had to speak to Lendi.

She must now ask her advice although she felt despairingly that it was impossible for Lendi to find an answer to her problem.

Della rode along the same path she had ridden this morning. She turned into the field where the caravans were parked, but there seemed to be no one about.

She suspected that the women might have gone to the village where they would sell their wicker baskets, which the Lees made more cleverly than any other gypsies Della had ever met.

Della reached the caravans.

Abram, who had looked after her horse that morning, came out of one rubbing his eyes.

When he saw her he smiled and she beckoned him. He ran towards her and she asked him to hold Samson.

"I will not be long, so let him munch on the grass."

As Abram was shy he did not say anything as Della turned and hurried towards the caravans.

The door to Lendi's was open and she ran up the steps and walked in.

The old woman was in bed but her eyes were wide open. She smiled when she saw Della.

"I expect you, Lady," she intoned.

Della was not surprised as she was aware that Lendi often knew that people would visit her long before they appeared.

She knelt down on the floor beside the bed as she had done earlier.

"I am in trouble, Lendi."

The gypsy nodded.

"I know, but the stars protect you."

Della had learned that the gypsies believed that every man had their own star and if as a woman she was protected by one it was an honour and a privilege.

"How can the stars protect me against this disaster? I am afraid, Lendi, very, very afraid of the future."

Lendi put her hand gently on Della's

"No reason," she murmured.

"But there is every reason," protested Della, "and I need your help to tell me what to do."

She thought as she spoke that what she was really asking Lendi was to save her as well as find a solution which would prevent her from having to marry Jason without upsetting her uncle.

She could feel, although Lendi's hand was cold, that there was life in it. It was difficult to explain, but the older woman's hand seemed to be giving her strength.

Lendi closed her eyes.

Della knew that she was not asleep but thinking.

Then Lendi said,

"Follow your heart. Be brave – not afraid. The stars – protect you."

The words came out very slowly one by one from Lendi's lips and Della knew they were inspired.

The old gypsy was communicating with the spirits who, she believed, belonged to the stars.

"Will I – have to marry – him? asked Della in a whisper.

There was silence until Lendi said very softly,

"Marry with your heart – you happy. Very – happy."

As she finished speaking she took her hand away. Della knew it would be a mistake to ask her anything more.

She bent forward and kissed Lendi's cheek.

"Thank you. I will do as you say and follow my heart!"

As she left the caravan she thought it was not going to be easy.

In fact almost impossible and yet it was what Lendi had told her to do.

Although it seemed her problem for the future was still as dark as ever, she was somehow feeling a little happier.

She gave Abram sixpence for holding Samson. She managed with a little difficulty to mount him and rode away.

She reached the wood and turned to go back the way she had come.

She was still conscious of the feeling of Lendi's hand on hers.

'I must follow my heart – ' pondered Della, 'but how and where?'

And if she did so, what would it mean to her uncle?

These questions were still turning over and over in her mind. At the same time Lendi had given her hope which she could not explain.

A hope which seemed impossible but almost, despite herself, she believed in it.

Believed it completely and absolutely.

She must follow her heart.

CHAPTER THREE

For the next two days Della was fully occupied arranging the dinner party.

She was determined that it should not be an intimate one at which Jason could speak to her about themselves as what she really wanted was to have a good look at him.

To see if he had improved – which was extremely unlikely – since she had last met him.

Her heart sank every time she thought of him, but equally she knew she must help her uncle.

He was wise and sensible enough not to talk about Jason when they were alone. Instead, they discussed every other subject which had ever interested them.

Della recognised, however, that he was worried and troubled. It made her more and more angry that the Duke, his best friend, should now have forced this virtually impossible situation upon him.

'It certainly does not seem very friendly to me,' Della grumbled to herself.

She finally decided that it would be a mistake to ask any of the young girls of the County to come to the dinner party.

They were all very charming and yet they were not so beautiful or particularly skilled conversationalists. It would be impossible for Jason not to compare them with the fascinating and erotic women he had known in Paris, which inevitably would be to their disadvantage.

Finally, after a great deal of thought, she asked a gentleman and his wife who she knew were extremely happy, so much so that people called them, 'the love birds'.

They were both in their early thirties and had been married for six years. To see them together was to know they were made for each other and nothing else in the world seemed of any importance to them.

She selected another couple who were older and they were friends of her uncle's. He had commanded a Regiment and retired to his family house in the County. He boasted a large family and his wife was still attractive and a very jolly woman. She was always laughing and obviously adored her husband.

'These two couples,' Della decided, 'will give Jason an idea of what is expected of him when he marries.'

That left her with a woman short.

She remembered Lady Southgate who lived in the next village. She was a widow having been married to a man older than herself and he had died of a tropical disease when he was in the East.

He had for a short time been the Governor of Hong Kong and Lord Lainden had stayed with them when he was in that part of the world. Lady Southgate was left without a great deal of money and so she retired to the country and took to breeding dogs.

She was much younger than her husband and Della reckoned that by this time she must be about thirty-six.

She was still very good-looking and even if she did

not amuse Jason, Lord Lainden would be delighted to see her and having entertained many guests as a Governor's wife she would be a delightful addition to any party.

Della spent a long time with Mrs. Beston choosing the menu. If nothing else she and her uncle must enjoy the dinner party and she consulted Storton about which wines would be the most appropriate for the occasion.

Whenever she thought of Jason she shuddered.

She could only hope when they did meet he would not be aware of her feelings about him.

The whole idea of their meeting seemed to darken the sky and yet the day drew nearer and nearer like a desert dust storm.

*

Della had to occupy herself during the afternoon as her uncle was working on his book, so she decided to go and see the gypsies again.

She wanted to have another talk with Lendi to make certain why her life in the future should not seem as bad as she feared.

She had, of course, remembered to send the gypsies the chickens and eggs she had promised.

This morning she had sent a groom with vegetables and jams she knew they would enjoy. Now she picked some flowers from the garden, which she could carry on the front of her saddle.

She walked slowly to uncle's stable.

The one horse she owned she had christened Apollo and he nuzzled against her when she entered his stall.

She always felt guilty that she had neglected Apollo as there were so many finer and more spirited horses at her disposal in the Duke's stables.

She remembered something as she patted Apollo. If things went wrong and she could not face marrying Jason, then he would be the only mount available to her.

'I will ride him now,' she resolved.

She told the old groom who had been with her uncle for years to saddle Apollo.

It was a lovely afternoon and the sun was warm on her bare head. She tried to feel the excitement that was always hers when she was riding.

Instead, however, she could only think that she was to greet Jason this very evening and after they had met, her uncle and the Duke would be expecting Jason to ask her to marry him.

It took her only fifteen minutes to reach the gypsy camp and as usual in the afternoon everything seemed very quiet and still.

However, as she approached the caravans Piramus appeared and stood waiting for her.

"Nice to see you, Lady," he said as she reached him. "I thinks you be comin' say goodbye."

"You are leaving!" exclaimed Della in surprise.

"Early morrow morn," replied Piramus. "We happy here – very grateful what – Lady and my Lord give, but must move on."

Della knew that 'the travellers', as the gypsies were often called, could never stay very long anywhere.

There were many legends as to why they needed to do so and one of them she knew only too well. The gypsies were said to have hammered the nails into the cross on which Christ was crucified and their punishment was that they should wander all over the world until He returned.

The Romanies were the true ancient gypsy race and they had first come to England in the reign of Henry VIII.

They had their own taboos, marriage service and unusual gypsy customs of death and burial.

The women were fortune-tellers, although few, Della was sure, were as good as Lendi.

She was upset to hear that they were leaving and she wanted to see Lendi right away, but it might have been more significant to talk to her after she had actually met Jason.

As she slipped from the saddle, she said to Piramus,

"I have brought some flowers for Lendi."

"She pleased, Lady, but this moment – asleep. Pity wake her."

"Of course I will not disturb her. I will just place the flowers on her bed."

She left Piramus holding Apollo's bridle and walked up the steps into Lendi's caravan.

As her son had told her, the old gypsy was fast asleep. Della was longing to talk to her, but she could not do anything so unkind as to wake her.

If Lendi was ill, sleep and fresh herbs were a better healer than anything else, which was the ancient gypsies belief.

She stood for a little while by the bed and felt as if she was reaching out to Lendi with her troubles.

In some strange way the sleeping gypsy heard her plea and comforted her.

Della could almost hear her voice saying again,

'*Follow your heart.*'

'That will be impossible if I am forced to marry

Jason,' she wanted to tell her.

She longed for Lendi to explain to her what she had meant by her words

The sleeping Romany did not move and finally Della had to turn away and leave the caravan.

Piramus was still standing where she had left him, patting Apollo.

"Fine horse," he said as Della joined him.

"You have met him before and he is a very dear friend."

Piramus smiled and she knew he understood. To the gypsies their horses were sacred. They were their best friends and they treated them 'as man to man'.

She knew that they obeyed their master's orders almost like a human being.

"I wish you were not leaving," she told Piramus. "Say goodbye to all your family and tell them my uncle and I will look forward to seeing you all again next year."

She almost added that she might, when they came, be in a different house to the one she was living in now. It was something she could have said to Lendi, but not to Piramus.

She merely bent down to hold out her hand.

"Goodbye, Piramus, and take good care of yourself and Lendi. You know how fond my uncle and I are of all of you."

Piramus bowed over her hand.

"Lady – very gracious, anything – you need us , we – come."

"How can I let you know when I am in trouble?" enquired Della.

"You call – we will hear."

Piramus spoke so positively that she knew he was telling her the truth from his heart.

She found his words very comforting. If everyone else failed her, the gypsies would still be her friends.

It was impossible, however, to put her feelings into words, so she simply said,

"Thank you so very much, Piramus."

He bowed again.

Della rode home, put Apollo into his stall and walked slowly into the house.

*

Storton had laid the table for dinner beautifully. The flowers she had picked earlier in the day looked most attractive and the silver candlesticks had been cleaned until they shone, while the glasses on the table sparkled.

"It looks very nice, Storton," said Della knowing well that he liked to be praised. "And I am sure the Duke will enjoy the dishes that Mrs. Beston and I have chosen."

Storton assured her that everyone would find the menu delicious.

For desert he had strawberries from the garden and grapes which had arrived from Wood Hall.

"Did anything else come with them?" Della wanted to know.

"Four bottles of champagne, Miss Della, two bottles of brandy and one of Cointreau."

Della felt herself stiffen.

The Duke was certainly making certain that everyone enjoyed themselves tonight. Equally she was conscious that he would not have sent them champagne if

Jason had not been one of the guests.

Food from the Home Farm and the greenhouse were one thing, but her uncle, who had a great experience of good wines, had always provided the best vintages at his table.

However, it would be a mistake to say anything in front of Storton so she merely congratulated him once again on the table and left the dining room.

Her uncle joined her for tea and deliberately talked about his book and the chapter he had just written.

Della became aware when he left her that he was almost as nervous as she was at what was to transpire later.

She went up to her bedroom to dress. She wanted to put on the plainest gown she possessed or wear something black.

'It will reflect the way I feel,' she thought.

Then she felt that she was being childish and stupid.

It would be a bad mistake to antagonise the Duke before it was absolutely necessary.

'What I will have to do,' Della told herself firmly, 'is to play for time. The Duke is in a hurry because he is afraid Jason will revert back to his old ways and this sudden penitence would be lost overnight.'

He would then very likely return to Paris and she was longing for him to do just that!

At the same time she must not be disloyal and it would undoubtedly upset her uncle if the Duke should realise that she was deliberately trying to avoid Jason – or worse still make him unwilling to marry her.

'Time! Time! Time!' she kept repeating in her mind. 'Time is what I need, but I must not appear to be reaching out for it.'

She forced herself to dress in one of her loveliest gowns. In fact it was the prettiest she had bought to wear in London before she was able to come and live in the country.

She had not been invited to a ball or party important enough to wear it so it had languished in her wardrobe and never been seen.

Now as she pulled it on she wished she was going to a glamorous ball in London where she might meet the Prince Charming of her dreams. A man who would love the same things she loved and understand what she felt about life.

'We would both know the moment we met,' she pondered, 'that we were meant for each other.'

She looked at her reflection in the mirror as she dreamed on.

'There would be no need for words as my heart would reach out towards his heart. After that it would only be a question of how soon we told each other of our love.'

But it was just a dream.

It was still in her mind until she was finally dressed and her hair had been arranged by Emily.

Her gown was white with just the slightest glimmer of diamante as if it was the dew on a flower. Emily pinned three pink roses at the back of her head, which was certainly very becoming and indeed no tiara could have been more attractive.

Round her neck she wore a singe row of pearls which had been her mother's and there was a bracelet to match them on her left wrist.

"Young girls should not wear jewellery," her mother

had always told her.

Yet Della knew that tonight she needed the help which only her mother could have given her if she was still alive.

'What would you have said, Mama?' she asked silently. 'Would you have told me that I must marry Jason or would you have come up with a brilliant and magical idea of how I could escape my fate?'

She thought she must ask the question of the stars.

Leaving the dressing table she walked towards the window to pull back the curtains.

It was not yet completely dark.

The first evening stars were shinning over the trees and later there would be a young moon climbing up the sky.

'Help me – Mama, *help me!*' Della prayed. 'I am so frightened. The Duke is a very powerful enemy.'

She felt that as she prayed that her mother had heard and understood. Della felt she could almost see her smiling at her and it was so comforting.

She turned away from the window and descended the stairs.

As she expected, her uncle had already changed into his white tie and tails and was waiting for her in the drawing room. The chandeliers had been lit by Storton and the room looked very welcoming.

As Della walked towards her uncle she realised that he was watching her intently and when she reached him he said,

"You look lovely, my dear, very lovely. I only wish I was taking you to a ball in London or dinner at Marlborough House."

"I wish that too, Uncle Edward, but we must try and enjoy ourselves this evening. I am hoping you will find Lady Southgate, who is sitting next to you, an amusing partner."

"I am sure I shall, my dear, and who have you placed next to Jason?"

It was a question that Della hoped he would not ask her and to her relief, Storton opened the door before she had time to reply

He announced two of the guests.

Della had thought it was too obvious if she placed Jason on her left. As she was the hostess she had seated the Duke on her right, as was socially correct.

On her left she had put the elder gentleman of the two married couples who she always found interesting.

She placed Jason on Lady Southgate's right.

On his other side she put the happily married lady and Della felt she was sure to talk to him about her love for her husband.

The guests now began arriving one after another.

As Della had expected, her uncle was delighted with Lady Southgate. She was looking very attractive and talking excitedly about a new litter of puppies one of her bitches had just produced and she was certain they would turn out to be champions. She was so enthusiastic that those who were listening became animated.

Everyone was laughing and talking when Storton announced,

"His Grace the Duke of Marchwood and his Lordship the Earl of Rannock."

The two men entered the room.

For a moment it was impossible for Della to look at

Jason and then when the Duke had kissed her on the cheek she found herself facing him.

Jason looked, she thought at first glance, rather better than she had expected.

He was thinner and Della thought that perhaps his unhappiness in his marriage had in some way improved him.

As he took her hand in his she felt the same as she had in the past.

It was as if she was touching pitch.

As she took her hand away from his she felt almost contaminated.

Fortunately her uncle was greeting him and talking about the old days when Jason had been a boy and they had hunted together.

It was easy for Della to move away as she now wished to speak to someone on the other side of the room.

Even as she did so, she knew she was trying to escape from Jason and what he had made her feel about him.

Fortunately dinner was announced a few minutes later.

Della had written out everyone's name and put the cards in front of their places at the table.

She had the feeling the Duke was surprised Jason was not sitting next to her. However, he did not say anything.

As soon as they had all sat down, she stated to talk to the Duke about his horses as it was a subject he always enjoyed.

By the time the first course was finished she was aware from the chatter and laughter at the table that the party was a success.

One thing was quite obvious, that Jason was trying, perhaps on his father's instructions, to make himself charming to everyone, especially to the two ladies beside him who certainly seemed to find him amusing.

Della noticed that the Duke kept glancing in his son's direction and he was obviously pleased with what he was observing.

Towards the end of the dinner, he enquired of Della,

"What have you arranged for us to do after dinner?"

"I thought," she replied, "that as no one would want to play bridge, which is always I feel a somewhat dull game, it would be pleasant to talk and, of course, have an early evening."

It was what she desired herself, but as an excuse she added,

"Uncle Edward has been working so hard on his book and I think it would be a mistake for him to stay up too late. It is something, as you know, he has always disliked."

The Duke smiled.

"Edward certainly had too many late nights when he was at the Foreign Office. I remember him telling me that the Germans could never be persuaded to retire to bed at a reasonable hour and the French usually went home when it was dawn!"

Della chuckled.

"I have heard him tell that story and that is why here we retire to bed early and rise early."

"Indeed you do," exclaimed the Duke. "When I looked out from my bedroom window yesterday morning just after I had been called, I saw you riding through the

Park and down towards the woods."

"I love your woods, Your Grace, I always feel happy in them."

"Then I do hope they will be always be at your disposal, my dear."

Once again she felt that a cold hand was touching her. He was warning her, threatening her, that if she did not do what he wanted the woods would be closed to her and so would his stables.

With an effort Della forced herself to reply lightly,

"I am relying on Your Grace to leave early tonight and then everyone else will depart too."

There was a pause before the Duke said in a low voice,

"I feel that Jason has not had a chance to talk to you this evening, so I will send him over to see you tomorrow afternoon. Shall we say about three o'clock?"

Della did not answer.

She felt it was unnecessary as the Duke knew she dared not refuse to see his son.

It was fortunate that it was now time for her to withdraw with the ladies and leave the gentlemen to their port.

Della rose to her feet and they followed suit as she moved towards the door.

"That was such a delicious dinner, Della," gushed Lady Southgate as they walked down the passage. "Do tell your cook how much I enjoyed it."

"I will not forget to do so," replied Della. "Like everyone else she loves to be praised."

"Of course," agreed Lady Southgate, "and I want

you to come and praise my puppies, they really *are* adorable."

"I am very much looking forward to seeing them and I am sure Uncle Edward will want one."

"I have already promised to give him the best of the litter and the Earl intends to have one too."

Della thought it sounded as if Jason intended to settle down, but at the same time she could not prevent herself from shivering.

The ladies walked upstairs to tidy their hair and powder their noses.

When they returned to the drawing room, both the married couples had asked her and Lord Lainden to dinner the following week.

They all sat down in the comfortable chairs and one of the ladies said,

"I was very surprised to see Lord Rannock here this evening. I had no idea he had retuned from abroad."

Lady Southgate laughed.

"The village has talked of nothing else since he arrived. It is only now that they have learned that his wife has died."

"And a very good job too," added the lady who had started the conversation. "From what I have heard about her it would be impossible for anyone to accept her, so he was wise enough not to bring her to England."

"I am sure he will settle down now and enjoy being at Wood Hall," continued Lady Southgate. "How could he be anything else in such a lovely house?"

"And, of course," agreed the other lady, "with all those wonderful horses."

She looked at Della.

"You do not know how much I envy you being allowed to ride them. Jimmy had promised he will buy me a new mount as a birthday present, but I feel we shall never be able to compete with His Grace's stables."

"I do not think anyone could," answered Della cautiously.

The gentlemen now entered the drawing room.

After a short while the Duke announced,

"As our host and I enjoy what can be called an early night, I am going to leave."

"There is really no hurry at all," said Lord Lainden quickly.

"On the contrary, Edward, Della tells me you have been working very hard on your book and I am quite certain you need your beauty sleep."

"There I must agree with you, but do have a nightcap before you go."

The Duke shook his head.

"No, I am taking Jason away."

He lowered his voice so that only Lord Lainden could hear as he whispered,

"I have told Della that he will call on her tomorrow afternoon."

Lord Lainden did not respond, he merely nodded.

The Duke began to shake hands with everyone in the party.

As he and Jason walked towards the door, the two married couples said that they too would leave.

Lord Lainden did nothing to encourage them to stay as he walked with them into the hall.

Lady Southgate was left alone with Della in the

drawing room.

"It has been a delightful evening," she was saying, "and you look so beautiful I feel you have been wasted on such a collection of old people."

"I am so glad you have enjoyed yourself," replied Della, "and I know Uncle Edward loved hearing about your puppies."

"He has promised to come to see them and so, as I have told you, has the Earl."

Lady Southgate paused for a moment before she added,

"I am rather sorry for him. I feel he has been hurt as only a man can be hurt when a woman fails him."

Della had not thought of Jason in such a sympathetic light.

Now it struck her that it must have been a shock for him to find himself so unhappy, especially with a woman for whom he had sacrificed so much.

She smiled at Lady Southgate.

"You always do say such nice things and find something good in everyone."

"I try to, although it has not always been easy."

Lady Southgate walked towards the door.

Della thought she was a kind and charming lady with a pleasant nature.

When they reached the hall the guests were still waiting. The carriages of the two married couples had come from the stables first. They said goodnight again and hurried into them.

"I cannot think what has happened to your carriage, Ralph," said Lord Lainden to the Duke.

"They might have had some trouble in leading one of my horses into the shafts," commented the Duke. "We are trying out a new horse tonight which we have never driven before and he seemed a bit obstreperous."

"What he wants," Jason piped up, "is to be firmly handled. I have always thought that Grayer is too lenient with your horses and this is just another example."

The sharp way he spoke made Della look at him in surprise. Then she remembered that he had always been a somewhat cruel rider.

He used a whip unnecessarily and always punished a horse that did not come up to his expectations.

'He would treat his wife in the same way,' she mused.

The Duke's carriage appeared at last.

Della had no wish to shake hands with Jason again, so she started to climb the stairs.

As the Duke stepped out of the front door, Jason turned back and hurried towards Della and took her hand in both of his.

"I will see you tomorrow," he asserted, "at three o'clock, so do not forget it."

He spoke insistently as if it really mattered to him.

The touch of his hands on hers gave Della the same feeling she had felt before – one of revulsion and almost horror.

With the greatest difficulty she did not snatch her hand from Jason's, but forced herself to promise,

"No, I will not forget."

Jason stared at her as if he was seeing her for the first time.

"It would be a mistake for you to do so," he murmured.

He turned as he spoke and hurried after his father.

Della ran up the stairs and into her bedroom. Only as she reached it and closed the door behind her was she aware that she was trembling.

If the Duke had threatened her, so had Jason. It was something she had certainly not expected.

"*How dare he!*" she exclaimed aloud.

She was suddenly very frightened.

She was frightened of Jason and frightened of the pressure which was being piled on to her. Frightened that she might, before she knew what was happening, find herself married to a man she detested.

It was then that she knew she must escape.

There was obviously no question of Jason waiting as she had hoped, nor of her having a chance to find some way out of this marriage without offending the Duke.

The trap was set and all she now had to do was to put her foot into it.

'I cannot. I *cannot* do it,' she moaned to herself. 'It is – too much to ask.'

She looked wildly round the room.

She almost expected the walls to open and that she would find a hiding place in them.

Then suddenly, almost as if she was being guided by a power greater than herself, she knew what she must do.

It was really quite simple.

She must be brave enough to follow what her instinct told her was the only solution.

She was standing irresolutely in the middle of the

bedroom when she heard her uncle come upstairs.

He knocked on the door and opened it.

"Goodnight, Della! That was an excellent party and everyone enjoyed themselves."

"Yes – I think they did," Della managed to say.

"And Jason is coming over tomorrow afternoon, I understand."

"So – he – said."

"That too is extremely good news. Goodnight my dear."

He closed the door and Della heard him walk down the passage to his own room.

She started to undress in a frenzy. She first snatched off her jewellery and next the gown she was wearing. She threw it down on the chair as if it was of no consequence.

She put on the simple dress she would have worn the next morning.

She crossed the room and sat down at the French Secretaire which stood in one corner and took a piece of crested writing paper from its leather box. She opened the blotter, picked up a pen and wrote quickly without hesitating for a word.

It was almost as if the words she was writing were being dictated to her.

"Dearest Uncle Edward,

I have to go away for a short time to think about what is being asked of me and recover from it all being such an unexpected shock.

I know you of all people will understand.

Tell the Earl when he comes, that I had very foolishly forgotten I had promised to spend a few days with friends and as we are travelling along the coast in their yacht, it is impossible for you to get in touch with me.

It you tell him you will contact him as soon as I return, there need not be any hard feelings between you and the Duke.

Forgive me, but this is something I have to do and it is too soon for me to be able to talk coherently with Jason.

My Love, as always

Your very devoted niece

Della."

She put the letter into an envelope and addressed it to her uncle.

Then she looked into the wardrobe room which adjoined hers for a laundry bag and found a large one in which Emily carried away the clothes to be washed.

Taking it to her wardrobe she filled it with the simplest of her dresses, adding her underclothes, light shoes and her hair brush.

After picking up the letter she had written to her uncle she blew out the candles and opened her bedroom door.

As she expected, most of the lights in the passage had been extinguished, leaving just enough for her to be able to see her way.

Walking on tiptoe she placed the letter on the carpet outside his bedroom door and then she proceeded downstairs by a side staircase, which led her to a door that opened into the garden. She undid the bolts and slipped through closing it behind her.

She hurried across the lawn and through the bushes which led her into the stable yard.

The old groom who looked after her uncle's horses would be in his cottage and fast asleep at this time of night. The boy who helped him lived in the village.

It did not take Della long to put a saddle and bridle on Apollo.

She fixed the laundry bag on the back of the saddle and took Apollo to the mounting block and climbed onto him.

She left the stables by the back gate so that if anyone was awake in the house, they would not hear Apollo's hooves.

She rode without hurrying, because there was no need, towards Long Meadow.

The moon had risen by now and the stars had come out. It was easy to find her way and the light from the sky made the world seem enchanted.

As she rode on, Della felt as if the Power which had helped her before in her life was guiding her.

She saw the gypsy caravans in the distance and there was a glint from the dying fire in the middle of the camp.

She was remembering vividly, as if Lendi was saying it aloud, that she must follow her heart.

It was just what she was now doing in her own way.

Her heart was telling her that it was utterly and completely impossible for her to marry Jason. She just knew when he held her hand in his that everything about him was bad and unpleasant.

There was, however, nothing she could do about it.

'I am running away,' Della told herself, 'and it is the only course I can take at this moment. I have no alternative but to follow my heart.'

CHAPTER FOUR

Della approached closer to the gypsy caravans.

As she did so, she saw to her relief that there was a man standing by the dying fire and she was sure it must be Piramus.

Eventually it was easy to recognise him and he was looking at her in surprise. He must have been wondering who could be approaching the camp at this hour of the night.

As Della drew up beside him, she lightly slipped off Apollo's back.

"Good evening, Lady. 'Tis late for you – to be visiting us," Piramus greeted her.

"I have come to you for help, my good friend, Piramus."

She saw him glance at the large bag on Apollo's saddle.

"Please, Piramus," she pleaded, "may I come with you wherever you are going? I will explain to Lendi why I have to run away, but there is nothing else I can possibly do."

It suddenly struck her that Piramus might refuse to take her. He could be afraid of her uncle's anger if she disappeared or, perhaps, as all the gypsies possessed clairvoyant powers, he might divine that she would also be antagonising the Duke.

To her relief Piramus smiled at her.

"Anything I do for Lady," he said, "is gift – from the stars."

Della was so relieved that for a moment she could not say anything. She just stood looking at him to make certain she had not been mistaken in what he just said.

Piramus, however, was more practical.

He started to remove the bag from Apollo's saddle and put it down on the ground near the fire. Then he led Apollo behind the gypsy caravans to where the horses were kept.

Della did not move.

She knew he would be taking off Apollo's saddle and bridle before tethering his back legs so that he could not run away.

She waited by the fire looking up at the sky, thinking that the stars were looking down on her and telling her she had done the right thing.

She was still afraid that the Duke would be angry and so would Jason when he called the following day and she was not there.

Yet she remembered her uncle's long years of diplomacy in far worse circumstances. His charm and tact would enable him to make light of her absence and promise that she would be returning in a few days.

For the moment Della could not think of anything that might happen in the future. All she was concerned with was getting away tonight.

She would go anywhere so that she would not be waiting for Jason when he arrived for her.

Piramus came back carrying Apollo's saddle and bridle. He put them inside one of the caravans which Della thought must be his.

Then he came to where she was standing.

"Lady share caravan with Mireli?"

"I would love to," responded Della, "and I only hope she does not mind having a companion to stay."

"Lady – honoured guest."

He spoke firmly and Della knew that none of his clan would dare comment on her arrival if he, as their Chief, accepted her.

Picking up Della's bag, Piramus strode towards the caravan next to Lendi's. Della realised that the gypsies always placed their most precious women, the old and the young, in the centre of the crescent of caravans with a man at each end.

They reached Mireli's caravan and Piramus went up the steps first carrying Della's bag.

It was not dark inside the caravan as the light from the stars and the rising moon was shining through the windows. The curtains were drawn back and light streamed through the door and this enabled Della to see that Mireli was asleep on one side of the caravan.

On the other side was an empty bed. Piramus touched it to make certain there were blankets on it and a pillow.

"Tomorrow – find sheets," he muttered.

"Thank you, thank you so very much," whispered Della. "I am very grateful and shall be quite all right as long as I can lie down."

"Go to bed Lady – sleep. We leave very early – no hurry for you."

He was speaking to her in a low voice and he did not wait for Della to reply.

He walked out of the caravan closing the door behind him, but there was still plenty of light for Della to take off her dress and her stockings.

Then she thought it would be too difficult to find a nightgown in the bag she had brought with her and if she moved she might wake Mireli. The girl had not stirred since she and Piramus had come into the caravan.

Della did not wish at the moment to make any more explanations as to her presence, so wearing her petticoat and underclothes she slipped under the blankets.

She placed her head wearily down on the pillow.

She had done it!

She had made the tremendous effort to run away and now she felt limp and exhausted.

The whole tension of arranging the dinner party and acting the role of hostess had been hard enough.

Worse still was meeting Jason and realising he was not only what she expected, but worse.

'I cannot marry him,' she told herself again and again. 'I know I cannot do it."

But this was not the moment for making decisions. She had made, she thought, the most sensible one in giving herself time.

Time to think, time to decide and time to scheme.

It was, she pondered, the stars which Lendi had told her were protecting her – the stars which had made her realise that her only chance of salvation was to run away.

Tomorrow would have been too late as the gypsies would have moved on and she could not think of anyone else she could have appealed to in her plight.

'I am safe here and very, very grateful for it.'

She must have fallen asleep as the next thing she knew was that the wheels were moving under her.

The gypsies were on their way.

It must be, she reckoned, very early in the morning as it was still dark and as she peered through the windows she could see that the stars had left the sky but the sun had not yet risen.

Beside the rumble of the wheels of the caravan, she could hear the other caravans moving too, but there were no voices to be heard.

For the first time she became aware that the gypsies when moving away from a neighbourhood always made sure they were not observed.

They came in silently and left the same way.

They did not wish to be asked questions or for people to follow them.

They were independent travellers making sure that, if it was at all possible, they were almost invisible.

Della must have dozed off again for when she awoke she found Mireli sitting on the other bed looking at her in astonishment.

"I did not hear Lady arrive!"

Della smiled

"You were fast asleep and Piramus suggested that I might share your caravan with you."

"You coming with us, Lady?"

"If you are kind enough to have me."

"But of course, Lady, it is very exciting you want to be with us."

"I am running away," Della told her, "and you,

71

Piramus and Lendi must hide me."

Mireli thought this was the most exciting news she had ever heard.

Later when they had stopped by the roadside for breakfast, all the gypsies clustered round Della as if they could not believe she was real.

"Lady really coming with us?" one of them asked. "People think – very strange."

"You must make me look just like one of you," suggested Della. "Perhaps if I wore a handkerchief over my hair, no one would notice me."

One of the older women laughed.

"Do better than that, Lady."

When they had eaten a hasty breakfast of the eggs Della had sent them, they moved on again and it was then that the gypsy women joined Della in Mireli's caravan.

"If you hiding, Lady," one said, "you must look like gypsy. I change hair."

"How can you do that?" enquired Della rather nervously.

"Make it – black," replied the woman.

"I do not want to dye my hair for ever. I will wear a handkerchief over it."

"We gypsies have dye – wash out very easily."

She left the caravan so Della waited. She had not thought when she ran for help to the gypsies that none of them would have fair golden hair.

Her eyes too could never be the dark colour of the Romanies. They were, actually, a very dark blue which at times seemed almost to change to purple.

Della had inherited her eyes from her mother and

she had so often heard people admiring them saying they had never seen eyes that colour before.

"I think if the truth be told," Della's mother had said, "they come from my ancestors. Our fair hair must come from some Nordic country that invaded Scotland in the past."

Della knew that whoever the invaders were they violated the women, which resulted in most Northerners boasting the fair hair and blue eyes of the Vikings.

When the gypsy woman returned she brought a dog with her, a brown and white spaniel and she made it lie down on the floor.

Then she painted one of the white spots on its fur with some dark liquid she had brought with her in a bowl.

Della watched her with increasing interest as she realised this was the dye the gypsy woman was going to put on her hair.

She felt it was very kind of her to take so much trouble, but she had no intention of remaining dark like the Romanies and she surmised that it could be months before her hair would gradually grow back to its natural golden hue.

The gypsy woman painted a white spot on the dog black. Then she waited for it to dry saying as she did so,

"This made from special herbs known only to Romanies. We use it when our hair is going white or does not shine."

Della felt there was nothing she could say and the gypsy too was silent.

Next she had placed her hand on the dark patch of the dog's back when she thought it was dry and asked Mireli who was watching intently to bring her some water.

There was a bowl near her bed where Della had already supposed that she and Mireli would have to wash. Mireli obediently poured a little water into the bowl and the gypsy woman dipped a flannel into it.

Then she rubbed the dark patch on the dog's back and to Della's astonishment the black colour was removed immediately. It took only two or three rubs to leave the dog's coat as white as it had been.

The gypsy woman laughed at the expression on Della's face.

"Lady think gypsy magic. It very old, old recipe of Romanies."

"It is wonderful!" exclaimed Della, "and I do think it is such a clever idea to make my hair black so no one could question that I am not one of you."

She had been thinking about her uncle as she watched the women. When he heard the Romanies had departed he might easily think that she was hiding with them.

It would not occur to the Duke, but Lord Lainden was a very astute man and not easily deceived.

There was just a chance, Della considered, that he would decide to fetch her back and would send the grooms to find her. They would certainly not be looking for a dark-haired girl, so she should be safe until she was ready to return.

'I know it cannot be too long,' she pondered. 'At the same time I shall have time to think about my fate.'

The thought made her feel apprehensive because, when she did return home, Jason would undoubtedly be waiting for her.

But she did not want to think about him at all at this

particular moment.

She allowed the gypsy woman to very gently smooth the dark liquid on to her hair and then she looked at herself in the small cracked mirror that was all Mireli kept in her caravan.

She certainly looked *so* very different that not even her best friend would recognise her and, because she was so unselfconscious, she did not realise how the dark hair now accentuated the clear translucence of her skin.

Her mother had always been told that she had skin like a pearl and when she thought about it Della was glad she had inherited it.

"Now you look just like *us*," trumpeted Mireli.

Yet there was really very little resemblance between Della and the dark skinned Romanies, although she did indeed look most attractive in her new guise.

They sat down and talked to each other.

There was no chance of moving into any other caravan until late in the afternoon and Mireli told her that when they were travelling they usually only stopped for breakfast and then enjoyed a big meal at six o'clock.

"Cook over camp fire," she said. "Better than little bites without substance."

Della laughed.

She liked the rather pedantic manner way Mireli talked. She realised it was because she was trying to copy Lendi, while she was taking her lessons in fortune-telling.

"Very interesting," Mireli told her when Della questioned her. "Tomorrow you come with me and listen to Lendi. Her very, very clever and she has learned from moon."

Della knew there could be no higher compliment

and although her eyes twinkled she did not make any comment.

Because the gypsies owned good horses they travelled further during the day than she would have expected. In fact she was not surprised to learn that they had already left Hampshire and were now moving into Wiltshire.

She only noticed how far they had gone after she had looked at some of the signposts they passed and realised they did not belong to her own County.

She understood only too well, however, that the gypsies did not like to be asked too many questions about themselves, their own language, their beliefs or their destination. It was, Della guessed, because of many centuries of persecution. Years of never knowing what would happen tomorrow made them as secretive as possible.

She therefore did not ask Mireli or the other gypsy women where they were going.

The woman who had dyed her hair came in several times to see if everything was all right.

Before they finally reached the place where they intended to stay the night, Piramus came to visit Della.

"Lady happy?" he asked, as if it worried him to think that she might not be.

"I am very happy, Piramus," enthused Della. "Mireli has been very kind to me and so has Ellen."

That was the name of the woman who had dyed her hair.

Della had been slightly surprised to find she had such an ordinary name. Then she remembered what her uncle had told her, when they were talking about the gypsies, that those who had come to Britain had deliberately changed their foreign names for English ones.

They had chosen the most ordinary local names possible. There were therefore now gypsies called Smith, Brown, Lee and Davis instead of their more exotic ancestral names.

Some of their women had also adopted ordinary English Christian names and Della thought it was a pity as they did not sound as romantic as their own, although she could understand it was much easier for them to move about the countryside.

*

Finally they stopped for the night and Della was informed that their new camp was on an estate very similar to the Duke's.

There were well-kept woods that she longed to wander into and wide fields that had been cultivated, whilst others had been put down to grass.

It was one of these fields that Pyramus selected for their camp with a confidence which made Della sure they had been here before and had been made welcome.

She had meant to look for the sign the gypsies always left outside any place they camped, which made it clear to other gypsies whether they were welcome or not.

She discussed this system with Mireli who laughed and told her that the signs the gypsies left each other were very significant.

A small cross meant 'here they give nothing!' Two lines across with one slanting down meant, 'beggars badly received.'

"What about a circle?" enquired Della.

"If it empty – generous people," replied Mireli. "A

dot in the middle – very generous people and kind to gypsies."

They both laughed.

"I think it is a very sensible idea," ventured Della.

"Especially for those," added Mireli, "who do not speak language very fluently."

As soon as the caravans had ground to a halt the men were unfastening the horses, while Della walked over to visit Lendi.

When she entered the caravan the old gypsy held out both hands.

"I told you were – with us. Welcome Lady and may you be happy and safe."

"That is just what I am sure I will be," sighed Della, going down on her knees beside the bed.

She kissed Lendi and continued,

"I was very frightened, so I ran away and then I was frightened in case you would be angry with me."

Lendi shook her head.

"Not angry, Lady. Very sensible and you – told to come."

"That is true. I thought it was either my mother or even the stars who told me I would be safe if I was with you."

Lendi smiled as if she was very pleased at Della's words.

Mireli came into the caravan.

"I was wondering, Grandmama," she suggested, "if you like to give me lesson while they prepare supper."

"I will do so," replied Lendi. "We must be ready in case you have to take my place."

Della knew she was saying that she might die and felt like protesting, but she thought it more tactful if she left the two gypsies together.

Before she could move, Lendi understood her thoughts and urged her.

"No, Lady stay and listen. Good for you listen."

"I would love to, Lendi, if Mireli does not mind."

"I like you be with us," said Mireli simply.

She sat down on the bed while Della reclined on the floor.

Lendi produced the Tarot cards from under her pillow and handed them to Mireli telling her to explain what each one meant.

Mireli did as she was told explaining what each Tarot card represented and making very few mistakes.

She was speaking in English, but occasionally, when it was difficult to find the right words, she would lapse into Romani.

Della was delighted to find she could understand a good deal of what she was saying. She thought while she was with the gypsies she should ask the others to talk to her in Romani to improve her knowledge of the language.

Mireli had been successfully through all the Tarot cards and this time Lendi produced a crystal ball, again from under her pillow.

It was a large crystal looking deep yet clear.

"Can you really see pictures in it?" Della asked Lendi.

"Sometimes," she replied, "but – important for – persons whose future you are reading to think. Easier – read thoughts rather than see them in ball."

Della thought it was a clever way of making sure the person whose fortune they were telling really did concentrate as he or she would be looking for what they wanted and what they were hoping for.

Lendi could then, quite easily, read their thoughts.

She was still telling Mireli and Della fascinating secrets when they were told that supper was ready, so the two girls hurried down the steps to see flames rising high in the fire round a large steaming pot.

Already some of the gypsy family were seated on the ground and they smiled at Della as she joined them.

Most of them, Della realised, were amused by her hair and there was no doubt that Piramus and the other men regarded her with admiration.

As everyone was hungry the gypsies did not talk while they were eating and the stew which Della guessed was a mixture of rabbit and chicken was delicious.

There were potatoes cooked in their skins to go with the stew and fresh vegetables and fruit to finish their supper.

Then one of the men started to play a violin. He played very softly so as not to disturb anyone nearby.

There was no human habitation to be seen and Della was certain they were camping on private property.

She did not like to ask outright where they were nor who had given them permission to camp on what was obviously a private field surrounded by woods on both sides.

In fact, when she went to bed, she still had no idea where she was and it was therefore very unlikely that her uncle would be able to guess where the gypsies had gone.

'Nothing is better for me at the moment than

secrecy,' she told herself firmly. 'And if I can talk to Lendi tomorrow, perhaps she will be able to help me solve the problems which are still with me, however cleverly I am disguised.'

It was a depressing thought and yet when she and Mireli blew out the candles in the caravan, she fell asleep almost immediately.

*

The next day was warm and the sun made the countryside even more beautiful than it had looked in the starlight.

What Della craved to do more than anything else was to ride through the woods, but she was, however, not certain if the gypsies were entitled to enter the woods. She felt it might be embarrassing to asked Piramus if she could and be refused.

Instead, when she had helped Mireli to tidy the caravan, she went to find Lendi. She had learnt by this time that the gypsy women took it in turns to look after her.

They washed her, tidied her hair, made her bed and cleaned out her caravan. The children picked wild flowers for her.

When Della saw Lendi, she thought, she was looking much better, although perhaps glamorous was the right word to describe her.

Della could understand only too well how exciting it was when the gypsies arrived in the local village and Lendi, looking like the Gypsy Queen, would receive them and tell their fortunes.

Now she was wrapped in a beautifully embroidered shawl with her dark hair well arranged and neat and she was wearing some exquisitely made gypsy jewellery that Della guessed had come from India.

"You look magnificent!" exclaimed Della when she entered the caravan.

Lendi chuckled.

"I am expecting a visitor," she said. "I can feel him coming towards me."

Della was curious, but again she considered it was unwise to ask questions.

Then Mireli piped up surprisingly,

"I suppose you thinking of – Marquis. He very kind to us last year."

Della's eyes widened and she wondered who this Marquis could be and if she had ever heard of him.

Then Piramus's clear voice came from outside the caravan. He was standing at the bottom of the steps.

"His Lordship's on way, Lendi," he called. "I see horse coming through wood."

Della found it impossible not to enquire curiously,

"What is the name of the Marquis you are now expecting? I suppose we must be camped on his estate."

"Marquis of Chorlton," replied Lendi. "He always kind to gypsies – we come – every year."

Della was trying to think where she had heard the name.

Somehow it was familiar, but she could not remember her uncle talking about a Marquis of Chorlton.

They had talked at one time or another about all the landowners in Dorset, Berkshire, Surrey, and Sussex, all Counties on one side or the other of Hampshire.

Della knew her uncle had quite a number of friends

in Dorset and the same applied to Berkshire, but she could not remember him talking about anyone he was friendly with in Wiltshire.

She was still puzzling over the name when Piramus called from the steps,

"My Lord here."

"As he is coming to see you," Della asked Lendi, "would you like me to leave?"

"No, you stay where you are," Lendi responded immediately. "But Mireli to go away, I not want him to meet her."

Della thought this sounded odd, but as Lendi was the most important elder of the gypsy tribe, it would have been very foolish to argue with her.

She therefore remained seated as she was on the floor beside the bed.

There were voices below and a moment later a man came up the steps into the caravan.

He was tall and had to bend his head to enter.

He was also broad-shouldered, but his figure was slim as if he was an athlete.

Then as Della could see him clearly, she realised he was very much younger than she had expected.

She had thought that because he was a Marquis and owned a large estate, he would be a much older man, perhaps the same age as her uncle.

The gentleman inside the caravan was obviously only in his twenties.

At the same time he was extremely good-looking. He moved lightly towards the bed and took Lendi's hand in his.

"I am very distressed," he began in a deep voice, "to hear you are ill. I have been looking forward to seeing you and I need your help."

"I always ready to help Your Lordship and we are glad to be back – with you."

"And I am more glad than I can say to see you," replied the Marquis. "I have been counting the days and been afraid you might have forgotten me in your travels."

"We could never," answered Lendi. "Now tell, my Lord, what is wrong."

The Marquis sat down at the end of the bed and as he did so he glanced, for the first time, at Della.

She felt he was questioning her presence in the caravan and she would have risen, but Lendi put out her hand.

It was a gesture which told Della without words that she was to stay where she was.

The Marquis paused and then as if he thought Della was of no particular consequence, he murmured,

"I have a problem, Lendi, which only you can solve."

"Tell me, my Lord."

"I have a niece, the daughter of my elder brother who, I expect you remember, died four years ago."

"I do remember. That first year we visited – your Lordship."

"That is right," agreed the Marquis. "Alice was only a child then, but you may remember her coming to see you on at least three occasions."

"I remember – very pretty girl. I told her fortune."

"I hoped you would remember," smiled the

Marquis, "because it is something I want you to do again."

"For important reason?"

"I was sure you would know before I told you, but yes, a very important reason. It is a difficult problem and one which I think only you can solve."

"Tell me."

"Soon after she was born Alice was left a very large fortune by her Godfather. He had no children of his own and was devoted to my brother. Therefore when he died unexpectedly from an accident, he left all his money to Alice."

Della was listening intrigued by the story.

"Because my brother felt it a great mistake," the Marquis continued, "for anyone to know how rich she was, he kept it as secret as possible. But after his death which was followed a year later by his wife's, it was impossible to keep people from knowing about Alice's fortune."

Lendi's eyes were on the Marquis.

Listening to him Della was conscious from his tone that he was extremely worried and she found herself wishing, even before he had finished his story, that Lendi would be able to help him.

"Alice is now nearly eighteen," the Marquis went on, "and she made her curtsy last month to the Queen at Windsor Castle. She is now undoubtedly the prettiest *debutante* of the season, but unfortunately she is also the richest."

"Be mistake," came in Lendi, "make her unhappy."

"It does not make *her* unhappy at the moment," replied the Marquis, "but *me*."

Della wondered why and almost as if she had asked

the question he said,

"It was inevitable that Alice should be pestered by fortune-hunters, but although I warned her constantly, it was impossible to keep them away."

"Fortune-hunters," repeated Lendi. "They clever – and unscrupulous."

"And very determined to get hold of her money," added the Marquis.

His voice was harsh.

"There one in particular – who worry you?"

"I knew you would understand. Yes, there is one and unfortunately Alice finds him attractive. It is not surprising because he is indeed a handsome young man, very glib and he pays her compliments which another man might find embarrassing."

"Your Lordship think niece – want marry him?"

"Of course that is what she wants," answered the Marquis. "That is why I feel, Lendi, you are the only person who can prevent it."

"How, my Lord suggest I do that?"

"Alice is looking forward to having her fortune told and what girl is not? I have been waiting to throw a party at which you will tell the fortunes of everyone present."

He made a gesture with his hands.

"You must be careful not to make it too obvious why you have been asked as the man pursuing Alice is no fool."

"You think he feel – you have reason inviting me to your beautiful house, my Lord."

"He would certainly think so, if you came just for Alice. That is why I must organise a party for perhaps ten or fifteen young people."

He paused for a moment and continued,

"Those who want their fortune told will be able to go into a special room after dinner, where you will be able to tell them all the wonderful things which are going to happen to them in the future."

"If they really wanting to know – "

"Exactly!" agreed the Marquis. "And I know without my telling you that you will realise if Alice is married entirely for her money, she will be disillusioned and miserable, as only a sensitive young woman could be in the circumstances."

"I understand. I understand. But my Lord, I – sick woman. Cannot leave bed. As you say be too obvious – Lady Alice come to me and I tell her – she in danger."

The Marquis put his hand up to his forehead.

"I was relying on you. What else can I do?"

"I have idea." Lendi held up one finger. "Someone take my place, do it cleverly. She here – listening to you. She understands – Lady Alice must be saved."

As she spoke she pointed at Della.

As the Marquis looked at her, Della felt herself gasp.

Then as she met the Marquis's eyes the words she was about to say died on her lips.

For some reason she could not comprehend she knew she must help him.

It might be difficult, it might be almost impossible, yet it was what she must do.

CHAPTER FIVE

As the Marquis left, again thanking Lendi for helping him, he raised her hand to his lips.

Della thought it was very kind of him and she realised how much Lendi appreciated the gesture.

When he had finally departed Della asked,

"How can you say I can go in your place? I am sure Mireli would be far better."

Lendi shook her head.

"No, Lady, you live in big houses – know important people. Mireli yet to learn about them. Very different telling fortunes of – villagers."

Della could see the sense in what she was saying, but equally she was frightened.

"But how can I possibly tell fortunes as you do?"

"Read their thoughts," said Lendi quietly.

Della was silent.

She knew that she was able at times to read other people's thoughts, but it would be very different with strangers.

As if Lendi could divine what she was thinking, she told her,

"Young people – all want love. They look into

crystal. You find easy to know – what they think."

"I will do my best," sighed Della.

She wanted to refuse outright, but doing so she knew would be most unkind to Lendi and it would be very ungrateful to the gypsies who had allowed her to run away with them without a word of protest.

How could she possibly refuse to do the one favour they asked of *her*?

Clasping her hands together she knelt in front of Lendi and pleaded,

"Give me a lesson, teach me, please, *please!*"

"I will," promised Lendi. "There no hurry. Moon help – better than me."

Della wanted to argue, but decided there was no point. All she could do was to attempt to learn from Lendi in two days, everything she had learned in a lifetime.

She was, however, thrilled when a little later she climbed out of the caravan to find Piramus waiting for her.

"Lordship when he left say if wish you ride in woods," he informed her happily.

"He said that!" exclaimed Della in astonishment. "But why?"

"He saw Apollo. Looks different to our horses. Lordship ask where I got him."

"I tell him Apollo yours. Now you have ride in woods and over fields."

"I cannot believe it," enthused Della, "but I am going to ride at once just in case his Lordship changes his mind."

"Lord not do that," smiled Piramus.

Because she was so excited at the idea of riding over

the estate, Della did not change her clothes. She quickly saddled up Apollo and rode into the large wood to the right side of where they were camped.

It was, she thought, as wonderful in its way as the Duke's woods, which she always thought of as hers. There were rabbits moving about in the undergrowth and squirrels climbing up the trees.

When she had ridden for quite a long time she found a pool just like the one she visited so often when she was at home.

It was actually larger and surrounded by trees which made it appear mysterious, but at the same time, as the irises and the kingcups were in flower, it was very beautiful.

She could imagine nymphs swimming in its cool depths and emerging from the water to seek the sunshine. She stood for a long time entranced by the pool.

It was only on her way back to the gypsy camp that she realised she was seeing the Marquis's house for the first time.

It was not very far away on raised ground, which is why she had not noticed it at first. It was large house, but not as enormous as the Duke's and although it seemed wrong to think so, it was much more attractive.

She guessed it had been built about 1750 and must have been designed by the Adam brothers.

The Marquis's standard was flying from the top of the main building. Between the house and the wood she realised there was a long stretch of water, which she reckoned, although she was not sure, was an artificial lake. She could just see that in the centre of it was a fountain throwing jets up towards the sun.

The spray glittered in the distance just like a myriad of precious gems.

'I would love to see the fountain much closer,' she mused. 'Perhaps I will have the opportunity when I go to the house to tell fortunes.'

She thought she would love to see the inside of the house as well as she felt certain it would contain unique treasures of the same antiquity as in Wood Hall.

She returned to the gypsy encampment and unsaddled Apollo with the help of one of the gypsy men. Then she went straight to Lendi's caravan.

"Lady had good ride?" asked Lendi.

"It was unbelievably lovely," answered Della.

"Message come – while you away. Party be on Thursday, day after tomorrow."

"His Lordship is obviously in a hurry."

"He need be," said Lendi simply.

Della felt sure she had heard the Marquis's name mentioned before, but could not remember where.

That evening after they had finished supper they sat round the fire while one of the gypsies produced a violin and played a lilting melody.

The stars filled the sky. The light of the moon was growing stronger and the trees in the woods looked dark and mysterious.

'Nothing could be more romantic,' pondered Della.

Everything was so beautiful that she was afraid it was only a fantasy in one of her dreams and it all might vanish without any explanation.

*

Yet the glorious dream was still embedded in her

consciousness the next morning and when she looked out of the window of her caravan, she realised that the one thing she wanted to do now was to ride Apollo again and because she intended to go a long way, she dressed in her riding habit.

Wearing only a pretty muslin blouse ornamented with lace and no hat she rode away from the camp.

She had noted that there were fresh eggs for breakfast and she was told they had been sent to the gypsies with the Marquis's compliments.

There was also fruit from his greenhouses and fresh strawberries and vegetables from his walled garden

"His Lordship is very kind to you," she said to Piramus.

"Like Lordship – your uncle. We very grateful. When we leave, Lendi blesses those who – so kind. We – sure afore we come again they find happiness."

Della hoped he was right, but she could see no happiness for herself if she was forced into marriage with Jason.

She deliberately did not tell Lendi how frightened she was feeling. She did not want to talk about it and was afraid to look into her own future. Perhaps Lendi would see that it was her fate to marry Jason even though she hated and despised him.

'I will not hurry,' Della told herself for the thousandth time. 'I must have plenty of time to think.'

She was desperately trying to find some way of escape and yet as she was so scared she did not want at the moment even to think of Jason.

She rode off.

There was no question of any of the gypsies

suggesting that one of them should accompany her as they appreciated that she wanted to be alone.

If she had been with friends of her uncle's they would have questioned her relentlessly and they would have been insatiably curious as to what she was going to do.

'The gypsies understand,' she told herself, 'as they could read my thoughts without hearing them spoken aloud.'

Perhaps not only Lendi but almost every gypsy could tell her exactly what was going to happen to her.

She was so frightened she did not want to know.

She just wanted for the moment to be happy with the nymphs and with all the other mysterious creatures she believed lived in the woods.

She realised that the gypsies believed firmly in fairies and they even thought that some of them took human form while remaining immortal.

The wood seemed even more entrancing today than it had yesterday.

She walked Apollo along the mossy paths until they reached the pool and as she drew nearer the sunshine came streaming through the leaves of the trees. It made the water glitter as if there was hidden treasure in its depths.

Because the scene in front of Della was so lovely, she dismounted and tied Apollo's reins together so that he could wander.

She stood amongst the irises looking down into the cool water and it was then that she unexpectedly heard the sound of a horse approaching. It was coming from the path on the other side of the pool.

Two seconds later the Marquis appeared from

between the trees.

He looked at Della.

Then just as she had done he dismounted and tied his reins leaving his horse free to join Apollo.

"I somehow thought," he began as he walked towards her, "that I should find you here."

"Why should you have thought that, my Lord?"

"Because I was quite certain it was where you belong and you wish to see, as I do, the nymphs swimming in the bottom of the pool."

Della looked at him in astonishment.

"I think you must – be reading my – thoughts."

The Marquis smiled.

"I realise that is your prerogative, but I saw you standing here and thought for a moment you were one of the nymphs."

Della laughed.

"Now you are flattering me, my Lord. It is just what I would like to be and I would swim right to the bottom of this lovely pool and stay there."

"And if you did so, what would happen to all your admirers? You would leave them heartbroken."

Della laughed again.

"As they do not exist there is no need for me to worry about them."

"Do you really expect me to believe that?" asked the Marquis.

Della shrugged her shoulders.

"It happens to be the truth and if I need a companion, my Lord, I am perfectly content with Apollo."

"I suppose that is Apollo I see over there. Strangely

enough he is most appropriately talking to Juno."

"Is he really?"

"He is indeed and like you I would rather be with Juno than any other woman I have ever met."

"You cannot expect me to believe *that*."

"Why not?" questioned the Marquis.

She moved from amongst the irises to where, beside the pool, there was a fallen tree which made a comfortable seat.

Without really thinking what she was doing she sat down and the Marquis joined her and as he did so he said,

"I can assure you I am very careful not to ask Lendi to tell my fortune. I am quite certain she would find me a suitable bride and I have a feeling her predictions would be even more pushy than those of my relations!"

Della chuckled.

"I can understand when you own anything as beautiful as this wood and your house which I can see in the distance, my Lord, that your family wish you to marry and settle down."

She was thinking as she spoke that this was exactly what the Duke wanted of Jason, although when he had married it had been a disaster.

Because even the thought of Jason upset her, she gave a little shudder and the Marquis asked,

"What is frightening you?"

"How do you – know I am – frightened."

"I cannot give you a direct answer," he replied, "but I know I am right and although you look like one of the nymphs from the pool and should be happy and carefree, you are, in fact, very afraid of something."

"You are – right," Della admitted, "but I do not want to talk – about it."

She thought as she was speaking how extraordinary it was that this stranger should be so knowledgeable about her.

And then she realised as she looked at the Marquis that he was extremely good-looking.

She suspected that his relatives were all determined he should be married as soon as possible as they would be worried at leaving him alone with his possessions however marvellous they might be.

"You are quite right," said the Marquis, reading her thoughts again, "but I am determined to enjoy life in my own way. You as a gypsy, who has always ignored convention, will understand my feelings as no one else."

"Of course I – understand," agreed Della. "You must never marry anyone unless as Lendi would say – you follow your heart and it is inevitable."

The Marquis smiled.

"That is exactly what I intend to do. I therefore made it clear that anyone who insists on talking about my future will not be invited to Clare Court a second time."

"Instead they will just talk about it behind your back."

"I am quite certain they will," the Marquis replied, "and of course young women will continue to be paraded in front of me like horses at a spring sale."

He spoke almost angrily, but Della found herself laughing.

"I can see it all happening and of course you are an irresistible prize, my Lord, for any ambitious *debutante*."

Only as she spoke did she think it was something a

gypsy would not have said, so quickly before the Marquis could reply she added,

"But I must not keep your Lordship talking if you have an appointment."

"My only appointment is with my woods, madam, and I am delighted that you should want ride in them."

It struck Della that, having said what she would do, he had deliberately come in search of her. It was, however, something she could not say to him.

Instead she said most sincerely,

"I cannot tell you how grateful I am, my Lord. As you are already aware woods mean a great deal to me and I always turn to them whether I am happy or in trouble."

"At the moment you are worried?"

She felt it was no use protesting any further.

"Yes I am, but I do not wish to admit it."

"I think what you desire," the Marquis told her, "is to be alone with the fairies and the goblins. Alternatively you might like to look at my horses."

Della's eyes lit up.

"Do you mean it?" she enthused. "Is it really an invitation?"

"If it would interest you."

"Of course it would, my Lord."

"Then come and look at them," suggested the Marquis. "I thought when I first noticed your horse that you would not ride anything so fine if, like most gypsies, a horse is more important to you than anything else."

"I can only say, my Lord, that I would be very honoured to see the horses in your Lordship's stables."

She tried to speak in a manner she thought a gypsy

would have done.

The Marquis rose and they walked to where the horses were looking for grass beneath the trees.

When Della gave a little whistle, Apollo came ambling towards her.

The Marquis did not say anything. He merely picked her up and placed her on the saddle.

He was very strong and Della extremely light.

As his hands held her waist she felt a little quiver. Not one of fear but something she did not understand because she had never felt it before.

The Marquis still said nothing. He walked to Juno and swung himself into the saddle.

There was a path out of the wood only a little way from the pool. When they were in an open field, without saying anything, they broke into a gallop.

Even as they did so Della, for some reason she could not understand, felt a desire to beat him.

She realised that as Juno was a mare she was lighter and slightly smaller than Apollo.

Then she realised that the Marquis rode exceedingly well, in fact better than any man she had ever seen.

When they reached the end of the field, he was just half a length ahead of her. She had been moving very fast and her eyes were shining.

As the horses came to a standstill near the gate she exclaimed,

"That was so exciting and I think Juno is a very beautiful horse!"

"So is Apollo," replied the Marquis. "And no Goddess, may I say, could ride him better or more gracefully."

"Thank you, my Lord. That is exactly the sort of compliment Apollo likes to hear."

"And his Mistress?"

"She is very grateful to your Lordship as well."

Della spoke humbly as one of the gypsies would.

The Marquis did not speak, yet she knew by the twinkle in his eyes that he was laughing at her.

'I must be careful,' she told herself. 'He must not think I am anything but one of Piramus's gypsy band.'

She had a sudden fear that if he suspected she was anyone else he might talk about her and in some unexpected way the Duke would guess where she had gone. He would then insist on her returning home so that she could meet Jason again.

The idea seemed rather far-fetched, but equally she felt nervous.

They had ridden, when they were racing, a little out of their way and now they turned back to climb up towards the house.

In front of the house there was a courtyard and a green lawn stretching down to a lake. This was a natural lake, which was joined further up by the house by an artificial one with the fountain in its midst.

Della looked around her, interested and intrigued by the house and its surroundings.

"Clare Court has been in my family since the reign of Henry VIII," the Marquis explained as if she had asked him a question. "The old house was burned down in the reign of George III and rebuilt by the Adam brothers."

"That is just what I thought, my Lord. They were such brilliant architects and their work is recognisable even at a distance."

Once again she thought she was being indiscreet. It was something a gypsy would never have said.

The Marquis however made no comment. He only led the way to the back of the house where the stables were situated.

One glance told Della that the stables were as up-to-date as those belonging to the Duke, and the Marquis's horses, although there were not so many of them, rivalled those she had been riding at home.

They walked from stall to stall with the Marquis explaining why he had bought each animal. He had been fortunate in finding several horses whose owners had not appreciated their value and were unique in their own way.

Della understood by the tone of his voice and the way he spoke how much his horses meant to him.

It flashed through her mind that this was how a man should feel, not like Jason who had wasted time and money with the type of women he had pursued in Paris.

As they reached the last stall with Della continuing to praise his horses, the Marquis turned to her.

"Now you understand why my relatives think I am married to Juno who you have just become acquainted with. And I prefer my stallions to those gentlemen who expect me to play cards for high stakes at White's!"

Della laughed because it sounded so funny.

"You are right, of course, you are right, my Lord, and I only hope you are clever enough to resist the temptations and traps they will set for you from time to time."

"Almost from day to day," added the Marquis. "But so far I have managed to escape."

"And that is what you must continue to do, my Lord."

"Is that your opinion or a prediction?" the Marquis wanted to know with a broad smile suffusing his handsome face.

"Both," answered Della, "but I expect the real difficulty will come when your heir has four legs!"

"That certainly will be something of a problem," agreed the Marquis, "unless like the Emperor Caligula, I marry Juno!"

Now they were both laughing, but at the same time Della hoped that he would not find it strange that a gypsy knew who Caligula was.

As they came out of the stable she said,

"Thank you a hundred times, my Lord, for showing me your wonderful horses and thank you once again for allowing me to ride in your woods. I think I should now return to the camp."

"I will see you tomorrow evening," said the Marquis, "and I have arranged a special place for you in the room next to the drawing room where you will look mysterious."

He smiled before he added,

"It will be impossible for the young people not to listen attentively to everything you have to say."

"I know your niece is called Alice, my Lord, but what is the name of the man you call the fortune-hunter?"

"His name is Cyril Andover."

"Is there anyone in the party you would like your niece to marry?" enquired Della.

The Marquis pondered for a moment.

"There is one very nice young gentleman, the Viscount Huntingdon. I think with a little encouragement he would ask her to marry him. He is not only the heir to an Earldom, but is exceedingly rich so it is no question of him pursuing her for her money."

"That is most helpful information, my Lord, and I promise you I will do my best to prevent her from making a disastrous marriage. Once she has realised what her husband is really like she would be utterly miserable."

She spoke intensely with a note of agony in her voice.

Then she became aware that the Marquis was looking at her curiously.

"I must go back to the camp," she said quickly.

She walked away from him towards Apollo, who was being held by one of the stable boys.

She thought she would reach him before the Marquis could do so, but he was quicker than she expected.

Without saying anything, he lifted her up onto the saddle and Della picked up the reins.

"Thank you once again, my Lord, for a fascinating and exciting morning. I have enjoyed every moment of it."

"So have I," answered the Marquis. "Goodbye Della, I am quite certain now you will not fail me tomorrow evening."

Della gave him a rather shy smile and rode off.

Without looking round she felt that he was watching her closely.

She had the strangest feeling that once again she was running away. Yet why it should be from the Marquis she had no idea.

It was just something within herself that told her she was on dangerous ground.

She sensed his eyes boring into her back.

Only when she was out of the garden and moving towards the woods did she feel she had really left him behind.

'He is very astute and I can understand why he has no wish to be married,' she told herself.

Once again she was remembering Jason and that any woman who married him could not fail to be utterly and completely miserable.

She was frightened with a fear that was as painful as if her heart was pierced with a dagger.

Only when she reached the woods did she feel as if the sun was shining again.

*

As she rode into the camp she noticed that Piramus was waiting for her.

"I have had a wonderful morning," she told him. "I have seen all his Lordship's horses and they are magnificent."

"So I hear," replied Piramus. "I've seen 'em in the fields and those 'is Lordship rides, but I am not asked into stables."

Della thought this could be embarrassing and asked quickly,

"Is Lendi awake? Can I see her?"

"She waiting for you, Lady."

He took Apollo from her and she knew he would take off his saddle and bridle.

Della thanked him and hurried up the steps into Lendi's caravan.

"I hear you go out – early," the old woman commented as she approached.

"I went riding because it is so exciting being in the woods. I met the Marquis and he took me to the stables to see his magnificent horses."

"That what I think you – doing," nodded Lendi.

Della sat down on the floor.

"It was very strange," she mused, "but I thought I could read his thoughts. I have read other peoples, but never so clearly or so correctly."

"Lordship – clever man."

"I know. He was telling me how he is determined not to marry. It seems a pity, but equally I am sure he is much happier on his own."

"He waits, find his star – like you."

"That is just what I want, dear Lendi, but perhaps it is something I will never find."

"You – find."

Della thought she did not understand.

Jason was waiting for her!

In two or three days time she would have to return home for the gypsies would not keep her for ever and however much she might fight against Jason mentally, physically she would have to help her uncle or too soon both of them would face the anger and revenge of the Duke.

She did not say anything, but Lendi murmured softly,

"Trust your star! Follow – your heart!"

"How can I follow my heart?" demanded Della almost crossly. "If it does not know in which direction to go? There appears to be only one way out of this mess."

Lendi smiled.

"You trust moon. If not believe then – things go wrong."

Della knew that Lendi believed in every word she was saying. But however long she stayed away she would eventually have to return to face her fate.

Perhaps by the end of this very week!

Even that would seem too long to the Duke and once again Della was asking herself frantically what she should do. She sat in silence for some time before realising that Lendi had fallen asleep.

Della tiptoed out of the caravan and walked to her own.

Mireli was not there. She thought she would be with the other gypsy women preparing a light meal for everyone to eat in the middle of the day.

'Tonight,' Della thought to herself, 'I must ask the man who plays the violin to play dance music. Then perhaps Mireli will dance round the fire, because tomorrow night I shall not be here.'

She was not looking forward to the visit to Clare Hall as it would be difficult to avoid making mistakes and even more difficult to accomplish exactly what the Marquis wanted her to achieve.

She could understand him wishing to save his niece from a fortune-hunter, but was it necessary for her to be a part of the plan.

She was labouring with such a tremendous problem of her own.

'I am being selfish,' she mused. 'But it is all too much when I am in such a terrible predicament. In fact it is really impossible for me to think of anything else.'

She ate the food the gypsy women had made for their luncheon, which was all very informal as the men did not bother to sit down. They ate either standing up or while they were grooming the horses.

Afterwards the women made off to the village carrying their wicker baskets, clothes pegs and other items they wanted to sell.

Eventually Della found herself alone.

Instinctively, without really thinking why she did so, she mounted Apollo and trotted again through the wood to the pool.

She had just reached her destination when she realised that the Marquis was coming in the other direction.

She drew in Apollo and waited for him to join her.

"I thought I would find you here," he called, "and I have a suggestion to make."

"What is it, my Lord?" asked Della.

"My niece and the other guests who are staying with me have gone out for the afternoon and I thought it might amuse you to see round the house."

"I would love to!" exclaimed Della.

"I thought what would really interest you," continued the Marquis, "are my pictures of horses, which is a collection started by my father and which I have added to quite considerably."

"Stubbs, Herring, Fernley and Pollard?"

The Marquis chuckled.

"I thought you would know them, although how, as a gypsy you are so knowledgeable, I have no idea."

"Perhaps it is because we have travelled so much," came in Della quickly, "and we have accumulated in our minds more than most people."

"And very much more than anyone I have met of your age," remarked the Marquis.

She did not answer him and after they had ridden a little further in silence he said,

"You might look like a gypsy, but you do not speak like one."

Della had already thought of an answer to this line of inquisition.

"I was fortunate enough to be looked after and taught by someone who, more or less, wanted to adopt me."

She thought as she spoke it would be difficult for him to query this answer.

"That is a good explanation and of course it makes you outstanding among the gypsies, even those as clever as Lendi."

"Lendi and all the gypsies, my Lord, prefer to talk in their own language. Therefore they do not take the trouble to speak the same English as you and I."

"You are an exception to every rule, but I still find it very strange that you should know so much and you can speak so perfectly."

"Then you must be aware, my Lord, that the gypsies come from the East, especially from India and Egypt and they believe in the Wheel of Rebirth or if you prefer the English word – reincarnation."

"Have you any idea who you were in your last life?"

he asked her.

"Whoever it was I could not have progressed as I should have, so I have been sent back as an ordinary gypsy."

She spoke lightly as this was rather a difficult conversation as she did not want the Marquis to be in any way suspicious.

"Hardly an ordinary gypsy," he commented, "but a very extraordinary one who I find most interesting."

"If you are putting me under your microscope, my Lord," asserted Della, "I shall ride away and not help you tomorrow evening. As it is I do not wish you to be curious about me or to read my thoughts."

"Now you must be aware that you are asking the impossible of me," answered the Marquis. "You have puzzled me ever since I first saw you sitting on the floor of Lendi's caravan."

He paused for a moment.

"I find it both intriguing and amusing to find you so different in every way to what I might have expected."

"Perhaps what you expected is what I would find somewhat rude and uncomplimentary. I would suggest, my Lord, we change the conversation."

"But of course. I have no wish to embarrass you, Della, but may I say I find you very mysterious and as difficult to explain away as the nymphs in the pool or the ghost that has been seen in the house by my ancestors for the last three hundred years."

"Then that explains everything," smiled Della with satisfaction. "I am a ghost come back from the past not to haunt you, but to help you. In fact you should be very grateful!"

CHAPTER SIX

Next morning Della was not really upset, only a little disappointed.

A message came from Clare Court that there was to be no riding in the woods today. She had not thought of it before, but she realised the Marquis was being sensible as it would be a mistake for her or any other gypsy to be seen before the dinner party.

As he had said, if his niece was not suspicious, the fortune-hunter might be.

It was a lovely day and Della longed to have a good gallop on Apollo, but it was forbidden. She had, however, plenty to do in having a last lesson with Lendi.

She held the crystal ball in her hand and they went over and over all the things she might sense a man or a woman was thinking.

"No hurry," said Lendi. "Wait – stars give you – answer."

"I only hope you are right and they are listening to my prayers that they will not forget me."

"That – not happen," Lendi told her firmly.

The groom who had brought the message about the woods had also informed Piramus that a carriage would come for the fortune-teller at eight o'clock.

At first Della thought this was a rather strange development.

She expected the dinner party would start at that hour, but when she reasoned it out, she realised that the Marquis was giving her time.

First to settle herself in the room he had prepared for her while the party was in the dining room and secondly that she would not be observed entering the house.

It would be a mistake for her to be seen until she was ready to receive those who wished to know their future.

She was not surprised when Lendi wanted her to dress in plenty of time. So she washed in her own caravan and then wearing only her dressing gown, she slipped back again into Lendi's.

On Lendi's instructions, Mireli and Ellen made up her face, accentuating her eyes and making them larger than they were already.

They darkened her eyelashes and applied lashings of powder, rouge and lip-salve. These were embellishments Della had never used on her face in her entire life.

When she looked in the mirror she thought it would be hard for her uncle to recognise her now.

She did not look in the least like a young girl of only eighteen.

It was when they had reached this stage that she saw the clothes she was to wear for the first time. They were, she learned, Lendi's *very* best.

The gown was of a very fine gold silk which shone with every movement she made. Over it was a gauze veil which fell from her head to her feet, held in place by a gold band in the centre of which was embroidered a strange emblem.

It had belonged, she was told, to a famous Indian fortune-teller.

Della had already seen some of Lendi's Indian jewellery and now everything she owned was at her disposal.

There was a necklace fashioned with small stones into an exquisite pattern. There were ear-rings, bracelets and rings to match, and each piece, Della thought, was lovelier than the last.

When she was wearing them all she felt like an Indian Princess.

She gathered from Lendi that they had been handed down for many generations. Her great-great-grandmother had brought them to Europe when she came from India.

By the time Della was finally dressed, she felt as excited as a *debutante* attending her first ball.

This was such an adventure and the mere fact that she looked so different in every way made it unbelievably thrilling.

She looked at herself in the mirror, as Lendi kept a large one in her caravan. It would be impossible, Della considered, for anyone she knew to recognise her.

The carriage arrived. It was a closed one drawn by two horses and all the gypsies came to see her off.

"Good luck. The stars guide you," urged Piramus comfortingly, as he helped her into the carriage.

There was a cheer as the horses started off and Della knew that the gypsies would wave until the carriage was out of sight.

She was longing to see the inside of the Marquis's house, but still she could not help feeling nervous. It would be ghastly if she made a mistake and let the

Marquis down.

As they trotted up the drive she said a little prayer.

Not to the moon or the stars, but to her own God and the Saints her mother always prayed to.

The front of the house was lit by huge torches on each side of the door and there was a red carpet down the steps.

As Della walked quickly up the steps she saw two footmen waiting in the hall to receive her.

She reckoned that if the Marquis did not wish anyone to see her arrive she should have gone to a back door. There was, however, no one to notice her as she was taken across the hall and down a wide passage.

She walked slowly because she wanted to look at the pictures hanging on the walls, the many antique chests and all the Marquis's beautiful furniture.

The footman ahead of her opened a door and she entered what she recognised to be the drawing room where three magnificent crystal chandeliers were blazing with hundreds of candles.

There were carved and gilded pieces of furniture which she appreciated had been designed by the Adam brothers.

Everywhere there was a profusion of flowers and it was undoubtedly one of the most beautiful rooms she had ever seen.

The footman walked straight through the drawing room and opened a door at the far end and Della knew before she reached it that this was the anteroom the Marquis had mentioned to her.

When she entered it was very different from anything she could have anticipated.

The Marquis had erected what looked almost like a tent. It was made of a thin dark blue gauze that was sprinkled all over with golden stars.

Beneath the tent there was a throne-like chair where Della guessed she was expected to sit.

In front of the chair was a small table covered with what was obviously an Indian cloth, embroidered, not only with silk, but with gems that sparkled in the candlelight.

"Be there anything you require, madam?" asked the footman.

"I am sure I have everything I need, thank you," replied Della.

Looking round Della thought how clever the Marquis had been.

It would be impossible for any young girl or even a man for that matter not to be intrigued. They could all consult the fortune-teller who was treated as if she was an Oriental Princess.

Della sat down in the chair and placed Lendi's crystal ball on the table.

It seemed to catch the light of the candles and as Della looked into its depths she thought she saw figures moving in it.

Then she told herself that she was just being imaginative, but when she held the crystal ball in her hand, she felt that it somehow vibrated to her.

She tried to remember everything that Lendi had taught her.

It was not long before she heard voices coming from the drawing room. The ladies must have left the dining room.

She thought they must have started dinner earlier than she expected and now the moment had come which would be a test of her brains and her ability.

She just wondered a little nervously if the Marquis would make her aware which among his guests was Alice, the Viscount, and the fortune-hunter.

She need not have worried.

The Marquis brought the guests in to her after the gentlemen had finished their port.

He introduced his guests emphasising their names so that it was impossible for her to make a mistake.

To begin with he was sensible enough to bring her two young women one at a time and Della thought they must have come from London as they seemed more sophisticated than country girls would have been.

To her relief she found it quite easy to tell them what they wanted to know and when each one left they thanked her for being so wonderful.

"She is marvellous!" she heard one girl exclaim as she walked back into the drawing room.

The Marquis next brought her another girl who obviously came from the country and after her came a young man.

Della was intelligent enough to realise that the one thing he wanted was to win a certain race. One of his horses was scheduled to run at the end of the week and she assured him there would be no difficulty in his horse passing the winning post first. He went away smiling happily.

She had told eight fortunes before the Marquis brought her Alice and he was shrewd enough not to introduce her as his niece.

Instead as he entered the room he said,

"We have still quite a lot of people waiting to consult Madam Lendi so you must not take too long, Alice."

"I want to hear everything she has to tell me, Uncle Kelvin," replied Alice firmly. "So the others will just have to wait."

The Marquis smiled at her, but he did not argue.

As soon as he left the room, Della began,

"Take the crystal ball in your hands, young lady, and think of what you wish to know and the stars which are watching you will bring you the right answer."

Alice did as she was told.

Della thought she was a very attractive girl. In fact, pretty enough not to need a large fortune for her to be a success.

Then heeding the Marquis's words, she told Alice that she was in danger.

"There is a gentleman," she said, "who has a honeyed tongue, but it belies his nature. He is stalking you like a sportsman will stalk a stag, but his heart is not in the right place. If you listen to him he will not bring you happiness but tears."

She realised Alice was listening intently to her as she continued,

"There is another gentleman who is favoured by the moon as being upright, strong and brave. At the same time he is quiet, modest and a little shy. He does not blow his own trumpet. You should encourage him because he will offer you what it is impossible for the first man to do."

"What is *that*?" Alice asked breathlessly.

"A true heart and the adoration that every woman hopes to receive from a man she might consider as her husband."

"But he has not asked me – "

"He is shy and afraid of being hurt. Even the strongest and most powerful of men can be made to feel humiliated if the woman they love is unkind or indifferent to them."

She paused for a moment.

"Hold out your hand or better still give him your heart. He is the man who will make you happy while the other who talks glibly will give you only disappointment and tears."

Della elaborated the story a little more and then lent back in her chair as if she was exhausted.

"I can see only too clearly," she resumed. "You stand at the crossroads. Be careful, very careful indeed, that you do not travel in the wrong direction."

She knew when Alice had left her she had given the girl something to think about.

After she had seen two other girls, the Marquis brought in the Viscount.

He was easy.

Della told him 'a faint heart never won a fair lady' and if he did not sweep the woman he loved off her feet, he would lose her.

"I am afraid of frightening her," whispered the Viscount.

"Women are not frightened by real love," added Della. "Show her your heart, tell her what she means to you and I do not think you will be disappointed."

The Viscount was delighted.

"You have given me hope and courage," he said. "Thank you, madam, I am so very grateful."

He bowed before he left the room.

Della was not at all surprised when after she had prophesied for two more women, the Marquis brought in Cyril Andover, the fortune-hunter.

There was no need for her to look into the crystal ball as Della became instantly aware of his vibrations as soon as he came into the room.

In many ways they were the same as Jason's.

She told him that he would make a great mistake in his life if he married while he was still so young.

"There are many good things coming to you in the future," Della told him, "but they are not yet within sight. Watch for them and be careful you do not miss them when they do appear because it will bring you riches and a position in life you have never had before."

"I cannot imagine what they can be," muttered Cyril.

"You must not be impatient. The stars cannot be hurried nor can the moon. If you take the wrong step now it will be something you will regret for the rest of your life."

She had at least, she recognised, given him food for thought.

Then the Marquis came to tell her that there were no more guests to consult her, so he thanked her formally for having made his party so successful.

The butler escorted Della from the anteroom into the hall and the carriage that had brought her to the house was waiting to take her back to the gypsy camp.

'Tonight has been,' thought Della, 'quite an

experience.'

At the same time she wished she could have seen more of the house especially the Marquis's equestrian pictures.

'Perhaps one day I can pay a visit to Clare Hall when there is no party,' she said to herself as she drove home.

But she thought it was unlikely as the Marquis had gone to Lendi for help, which she had now given him and perhaps he would now have no further interest in the gypsies or in her.

She did not know why but when the carriage reached the caravans she felt depressed.

One of the gypsies opened the door and as he did so the groom lent towards her from the driving seat and called,

"'Is Lordship asked I to tell you that I'm to fetch you tomorrow evenin' at a quarter-to-eight."

Della looked at him in astonishment.

"Tomorrow evening?"

"Aye," replied the driver. "I thinks as how 'is Lordship be havin' another party."

Della wanted to ask him for more information, but it was unlikely he would know any more. And it would be wrong to question one of the Marquis's servants, so she therefore thanked him for driving her back.

She hurried to the caravan she shared with Mireli, having forgotten that Mireli would not be there. As Della was likely to be back late she had said she would sleep with Lendi.

Della was glad to be alone.

Quickly taking off all Lendi's jewellery and the

elaborate gown she climbed into bed.

She was actually very tired. The huge effort of concentrating on so many young people, especially Alice and the Viscount, had been exhausting.

Almost as soon as her head touched the pillow she was asleep.

*

When she woke the following morning it was nearly midday.

No one had disturbed her and she had missed breakfast, but there was a little bowl of fruit by her bed and she guessed that Mireli must have put it there for her.

She dressed quickly and ran to Lendi's caravan.

The old gypsy was delighted to see her.

"What happened," she asked. "You do well? Not nervous?"

"I hope I did well," replied Della, "but I kept thinking you would have done much better."

"I sure you exactly – what his Lordship required."

"The sad thing will be," said Della wistfully, "that we will never know the end of the story. Alice is unlikely to announce her engagement before we move on and therefore I shall remain curious for the rest of my life as to whether I have been successful or failed to solve his Lordship's problem."

Lendi laughed.

"You see his Lordship again – very soon."

"Is that a prediction?"

Lendi nodded.

She was quite right.

In the afternoon the Marquis unexpectedly appeared

in the camp.

The gypsy women had all gone down to the village and most of the men had left with them. Lendi was asleep.

Della was sitting on the steps of her caravan in the sunshine.

She heard the sound of a horse approaching and to her surprise she saw the Marquis come riding from the direction of the woods.

He pulled in his horse when he reached Della.

"I have come to tell you," he began, "to come in an ordinary evening gown when you dine with me tonight. There will be no one who will ask you to tell their fortunes."

"In which case why do you wish me to dine with you?" asked a mystified Della.

"I will tell you later," replied the Marquis. "I cannot speak now, in case the young people who are roaming over the grounds see me. Alice thinks there was some reason for what you said to her last night."

"I only hope she will do what I asked her to do."

"She is thinking about it, I am very aware of that and the Viscount is being very attentive. In fact they are boating on the lake at this very moment, much to the annoyance of the fortune-hunter."

"Oh, I am so glad! Very glad!" exclaimed Della.

The Marquis smiled, turned his horse round and took off his hat.

"Until this evening," he called and rode away.

Della stared after him in complexity.

If he did not want her to tell fortunes then why had he invited her to Clare Court.

She was very willing to go, but it all seemed very strange.

She had fortunately packed into her bag a simple little gown that she had bought when she was in London. It was certainly a dramatic contrast to the fabulous clothes she had worn last night.

When she called to say goodnight to Lendi, the old gypsy told her,

"You look very pretty, Lady. Prettier than you look – as impersonation of me!"

"I quite fancied myself as an Indian Princess!" sighed Della.

Lendi laughed.

"You much more lovely as – self."

Della looked in Lendi's large mirror.

"I so wish it was true, Lendi!"

She was wondering who else would be present at the dinner party. She did not imagine it would be any of the young girls who had been there last night.

Yet if not, why should the Marquis have asked her?

She puzzled over this dilemma all the time she was being driven back to Clare Court.

The butler received her at the front door and she followed him down the passage to the drawing room as she had done last night.

Having asked her name he opened the door and announced as Della had told him,

"Miss Della, my Lord."

The Marquis was standing alone in front of the mantelpiece.

The previous evening, although she had been

agitated, Della had admired how distinguished he had looked in his evening clothes. He had worn a white tie and a cut-away coat which gave him a very athletic figure.

Tonight he was wearing a velvet smoking jacket like her uncle always wore when they dined alone. It was frogged with braid and was the deep green of the pool in the wood.

As Della walked towards him she thought it a strange coincidence that her gown too was green, although hers was the soft green of the leaves of spring.

"You have come," said the Marquis as she reached him. "I was half afraid that Piramus might suddenly have moved away without any warning or perhaps you had disappeared into the sky from whence you came to help me."

Della smiled.

"Have I really helped you?"

"I think so," replied the Marquis. "When my party left this morning, my niece Alice, instead of returning to London with most of them, accepted an invitation from the Viscount to stay at his home which is about ten miles from here."

"Oh, this is such good news," cried Della. "I am sure the fortune-hunter was not asked as well."

"No. He had to drive back to London, but he did not seem quite so annoyed about it as I had expected."

Della thought with a smile that was due to what she had said to him.

Then as if she had suddenly become aware of it, she enquired,

"Are you saying that all your party has departed? I thought you had asked me to dinner tonight because someone had been forgotten or perhaps wanted to hear more than I was able to tell them last night."

"They all thought you were marvellous, Della."

"I was so frightened of saying the wrong thing, my Lord, and when I got back to the camp I fell asleep the moment I climbed into bed."

"Tonight you need not worry about anything," the Marquis told her soothingly. "I thought after dinner you would like to see some of the rooms in my house and in particular the library."

"I would enjoy that more than anything, my Lord."

"No one could be as intelligent as you are without being an avid reader. I find it difficult to talk to any woman who never reads anything more serious than *The Ladies Journal*."

Della chuckled.

"That is a very scathing remark. I am sure that all the girls I was talking to last night have read romantic novels and were imagining themselves as the heroine."

"What about you?" enquired the Marquis. "Is that how you think of yourself?"

"I am not going to answer that question, my Lord, but I would love to see your library. I am sure it will be the equal to the wonders I have already seen in the rest of your house."

It was then that dinner was announced.

They were served with a delicious meal and Della felt it was as good, if not better, than anything she had ever eaten.

It was difficult, however, to think about food.

She and the Marquis, as they talked, seemed to be roving over the world and countries which fortunately she knew well.

The Marquis had started the conversation asking her about the origin of the gypsies. Did she think her particular clan came from India or Egypt?

"I have always believed myself," responded Della, "that all gypsies originated from India, but they have spread out, as you might know, in many different directions."

She saw that the Marquis was listening intently and she continued,

"Some came to Europe through the Balkans, others through Egypt and Africa, which I suspect, although a large number of people would argue the point, were those who eventually ended up in Britain."

The Marquis still appeared to be listening keenly to her.

At the same time he was looking at her as if he was digging deep into her personality.

His gaze made her feel shy and when the servants had left the room she asked,

"What are you looking for? What are you expecting from me?"

"So now you are reading *my* thoughts, Della."

"I would like you to give me an answer to my question, my Lord."

"I am not certain of the answer myself," the Marquis hesitated. "You are an enigma. Different from the other women I have met and, even though I read your thoughts, I find it strangely difficult to understand you."

"I am glad I can keep you guessing!"

They sat for some time in the dining room duelling, Della thought, with words which she found a fascinating exercise.

She was becoming aware that the Marquis was one of the most intelligent men she had ever met. And that included her uncle.

At last when for a moment they were both silent he suggested,

"Let me show you my library and then I expect you will want to return to the camp."

"I was very late last night so I had better not be too late tonight."

They walked from the dining room down a long passage past the drawing room. At the very end the Marquis opened a door.

The library was enormous and it must be the largest room in the house.

It was filled with books of every shape and size and its shelves were so cleverly arranged that Della considered it was the finest library she could ever imagine. In fact, she could not think what words she could use to praise it.

"It thought my library would please you," said the Marquis quietly.

"How can you be so lucky, my Lord," Della asked him, "to have all this, your horses and of course your magic woods?"

They smiled at each other as if there was no need to explain what the words meant.

Then the Marquis said in what she thought was an unexpectedly sharp voice,

"I think the carriage will be now waiting for you outside."

They walked back to the hall and Della picked up the light shawl she had borrowed from Lendi. As she was pulling it around her shoulders, the Marquis walked out through the front door.

He spoke to the groom who was waiting for her in the carriage.

Then as Della joined him he told her,

"I am sending the horses round the top lake so that you can pick them up on the other side. I want you to see the fountain at night."

"I would love to, my Lord."

They walked through the garden towards what she had thought was the artificial lake. It was very like the ones which were attached to so many of the Chateaux in France.

When they reached the top of the lake the fountain was just in front of them and it was throwing tall jets of water up into the sky.

It was then that Della realised why the Marquis had brought her here. It was obviously because the fountain in the lake was lit in an original manner she had never seen before.

In a way which he must have invented, there were lights under the water falling down into the exquisitely carved bowl. Lights too lined the edge of the lake itself.

It made the whole scene seem so romantic and almost a part of fairyland.

"It is *so* lovely!" she exclaimed, clasping her hands together. "Perfectly lovely."

"And so are you," murmured the Marquis.

As he spoke he pulled her against him and his lips came down on hers.

For a moment she stiffened in astonishment.

And then her body seemed to melt into his.

She had never been kissed before. Now the stars above them and the sparkle in the water all seemed to congregate in her heart.

She felt as if she had stepped into a magical world which she never knew existed.

The Marquis kissed her and carried on kissing her.

A very strange but wild and wonderful feeling rose within her breasts. She had become a part of an enchanted aura which surrounded them.

The Marquis was part of it too.

She knew that what she was feeling, he was feeling as well and it was a wonder beyond words.

It was a beauty which could only be expressed by the light coming from the sky and it seemed to Della that the moonlight was moving within both of them.

It was blessing them with its divine rays which came directly from God.

The Marquis kissed her forehead, her eyes, her cheeks and then again her lips. She surrendered herself completely to the strength of his arms.

The moonlight tied them together with invisible bonds from which they could never escape.

'*This is love*,' Della thought wildly.

The love she had known existed somewhere, if she could only find it.

The love which was sacred and which all people have sought but few were lucky enough to find.

'I love you – *I love you*,' she wanted to cry out to the Marquis.

Now his lips were on hers again and it was

impossible to speak. Only to feel an inexpressible wonder and glory.

Then suddenly he took his arms from her.

It happened so unexpectedly that she almost fell and she put out a hand to steady herself.

As she held on to the bridge she felt the Marquis was moving away from her.

She could not breathe and she could not see.

Then as she opened her eyes she saw that he had left her.

She was alone.

Alone looking at the fountain, at the lights gleaming like diamonds in the darkness and in the cold water just beneath her.

It did not seem possible that he had actually gone.

After a moment she came back to reality.

She looked round and there was no sign of him.

There were only the lights below her and the darkness on either side.

Slowly, because Della felt that her feet would not carry her, she walked to where she knew the carriage would be waiting for her.

She went almost as if she was walking in a dream.

A dream which had broken and she was by herself.

She stepped into the carriage.

The groom, who had jumped down from the driving seat when she appeared, closed the door behind her.

Then as he drove off, Della put her hands up to her face.

Could it be true, could it really have happened?

The Marquis had kissed her and taken her into a heaven of ecstasy and adoration only to leave her?

They drove on.

When they arrived at the camp she managed to step out and thank the groom for bringing her back.

"It's been a pleasure, madam," he said, touching his forelock.

She tried to smile at him.

Next she stumbled to the caravans where everything was still and silent.

She knew that Mireli was once again sleeping in Lendi's caravan and she was grateful that hers was empty.

Only as she walked up the steps and sat down on the bed, did she ask herself what had really happened.

'I love him – *I love him*,' she whispered beneath her breath.

It was the truth.

She had loved him since the first time she had met him. Because she had never been in love before she had not realised what would happen when she met him again.

Her heart seemed to turn a dozen somersaults.

It was then as she sat there in the caravan that she knew it would be impossible for her to see him again.

Even to look at him would be to betray the love she felt for him and which could not be hidden.

She understood why he had left her and disappeared.

Because they were so close to each other with their minds and now with their bodies, she knew what he was thinking.

As he told her, he had resisted the pressures and requests of his family that he should marry.

He had waited, as she had waited, to fall in love and it had happened.

They had found each other perhaps after a mission of many years of search.

Then as Lendi would say, their stars had met and they were one.

But she was a gypsy or so he thought and he was a nobleman and proud of it. As well he had no wish to be married as he had told her all too clearly.

It suddenly occurred to Della that he might offer her something else.

Something which would not only be humiliating, but would spoil what, for the moment, was the most perfect feeling she had ever known.

Whatever happened in the future, whatever she had to endure, no one could take that moment away from her.

The wonder she had known and felt when the Marquis had kissed her was hers for ever.

He had carried her up in to the sky.

She had been one not only with the stars but with the angels, who she had always believed in, and with the Gods she had always worshipped.

What was more, no one must besmirch it, or make it anything but what it was, the perfection of pure love.

All these thoughts coursed though Della's mind.

She knew almost as if a voice was commanding her what she must do.

'I must go home,' she told herself in a whisper.

There was some water in the china jug in the basin between the two beds. So Della took off her evening gown and kneeling on the ground bent her head over the basin.

She washed away the black dye the gypsy woman had put on her hair and it came away quite easily.

As she caught a glimpse of herself in the mirror she could see her hair was shining in the light from the candle.

She rubbed her hair until it was nearly dry and then lay down on the bed, not bothering to undress any further.

She knew that she must leave the camp, if possible before anyone else was awake. There was no reason why the Marquis should come here, but she was taking no risks.

She would go back to her uncle.

Somehow, although she could not work it out now, she would try her best to avoid having to marry Jason, which would be even more frightening and more horrible now than it would have been at first.

It may not mean so much to the Marquis, but to Della it was the door to a new world she had never known.

A world where love was sublime.

It was totally different from anything else and the only real importance in life.

The Marquis had given her a vision of indefinable love and exquisite beauty and she could not bear it to be spoiled or belittled.

As she had nowhere else to go she must return home.

Quicker than she expected, she noticed that the stars were fading. The moonlight had gone and there was, when she looked out of the caravan window, a faint gleam of light in the distance.

Dawn was approaching.

Now she could slip away and the quicker the better.

She bundled everything that belonged to her into the bag she had brought and put on her riding skirt.

She reckoned that it would be too hot to ride the long way she had to go wearing a coat so she packed that too and the dress she had worn for dinner.

She tied a pink handkerchief over her head. If there was anyone about, they would not see her fair hair.

Silently so that no one could hear her she crept down the steps.

She moved past the silent caravans to where the horses were hobbled, Apollo amongst them. It took her some time to untie the ropes which tethered his legs.

The gypsy men's fingers were stronger than hers, but finally Apollo was free.

By this time the light on the horizon had turned to gold and the first rays of the sun were sweeping away the darkness of the night.

Talking to Apollo in a low voice Della attached her bag to his saddle.

"We are going home, Apollo. I am afraid of what might await us, but we cannot stay here. I love him – Oh, Apollo, I love him – and because I will never see him again, I only wish I could die!"

She finished fastening her bag and as she did so she heard a step behind her.

She thought it would be Piramus and she tried to think quickly about what she would say to him – what explanations she would make for leaving.

She turned round to face him.

It was the Marquis!

CHAPTER SEVEN

For a moment they stood staring at each other.

Then Della realised that the Marquis was still in the smoking jacket he had worn at dinner and therefore he not been to bed.

Almost without meaning to she blurted out,

"Why are – you – here? Why – have you – come?"

There was a pause before the Marquis replied very quietly,

"I have come to ask you a question."

Della gave a cry and put her hands up to her ears.

"No! *No!*" she exclaimed. "It was so – wonderful, so – perfect – you cannot spoil it."

She turned away as she spoke.

She could not bear to look at him any longer.

"So wonderful – so perfect," the Marquis repeated. "That is just what I felt and that is why, my darling, *I am asking you how soon will you marry me?*"

Della became very still.

She could not believe what she had heard. It must be part of her imagination.

Then as if there was no need for him to wait for an answer, the Marquis picked her up in his arms and placed her onto Apollo's back. As he did so Della saw that Juno was just behind him.

She could not speak.

She could not think.

She was only sure that she was in a dream.

The Marquis could *not* have said what she thought he had said.

As if he realised how she was feeling, he mounted Juno and bent down to take hold of Apollo's reins.

He led the horse and Della away from the caravans.

Only when they were out of the field did he drop Apollo's rein and spur Juno forward.

There was no need for Della to do anything and as Apollo knew better than she what was happening he kept up with Juno. They rode in silence though the next field which led them towards Clare Court.

There was no way that Della could talk to the Marquis because the horses were moving so swiftly and yet if she had been able to speak to him, she would not have known what to say.

Could it really be true what he had just asked her?

How was it possible for him to marry a woman he believed to be a gypsy?

They reached the park and the horses moved a little slower between the trees. The stags which had been asleep hurried out of their way and next they were crossing the lake.

Della thought they were heading for the front door, but instead the Marquis rode under the arch which led to the stables.

He drew in Juno and Apollo stopped beside him.

There was no one about and everything was very quiet.

The Marquis dismounted and came to Della's side.

She looked down at him wanting to ask a dozen questions, but the words would not come to her lips.

He lifted her to the ground and released her bag from Apollo's saddle.

As he did so a young groom, rubbing his eyes, emerged from one of the stable doors. He looked in surprise at the horses and as he hurried towards them the Marquis took hold of Della's hand.

She felt a quiver go through her because he was touching her.

He did not speak, but drew her onto a narrow path with large rhododendron bushes on either side that led to the garden.

He moved very quickly and Della had difficulty in keeping up with him even though he was still holding her hand.

They stopped at a door which was unlocked and he walked in. There was a dimly lit passage with a staircase at the far end.

Still without speaking, the Marquis climbed up the stairs carrying Della's bag and she followed him.

He stopped before a large oak door.

"We both need sleep," he began slowly, "and later today we will be married."

Della gave a cry.

"How – can – you?"

The Marquis held up his hand.

"I know all the arguments my family will make and all the criticism that will come from your people because you have married a Gorgio. That is why I do not intend to listen to anything either you or anyone else has to say on the subject!"

There was a short pause before he continued,

"You are mine. You belong to me and I belong to you. Our stars are joined and there is no escape for either of us!"

As he finished speaking he opened the door.

Della saw it was a large bedroom in which candles were burning on the dressing table and beside the bed.

The Marquis put her bag down on the floor.

"Go to sleep, my precious darling, and I shall do the same."

He looked at her and she thought she detected a glint of fire in his eyes.

"If I touch you," he muttered softly, "I shall not be able to leave you. I am going to lock your door not only to prevent you from escaping, which I know in your heart you have no wish to do, but also to prevent anyone, including me, from disturbing you."

"But – listen," pleaded Della, "I must – tell you."

The Marquis put up his hand.

"There is nothing to say, my dearest Della. I love you and you love me and that is all either of us needs to know."

He looked at her again.

She knew without words how much he wanted to hold her close to him and how he longed to kiss her as he had by the fountain.

Then, as if he had to force himself to obey his own commands, he walked out of the room.

He closed the door behind him and Della heard the key turn in the lock.

She could not believe it had happened.

She stood staring at the door as if she felt it might open again and then she sat down on the bed.

Could it be true?

Was she dreaming?

Did the Marquis really mean to marry her?

She knew without being told that every word he had said to her came straight from his heart.

It was what he intended to do and no one would be allowed to prevent him.

She closed her eyes at the sheer wonder and ecstasy of it all.

He loved her as she had always wanted to be loved. So much that he was prepared to marry a gypsy woman who would shock and horrify his relations.

What was more he really believed that Lendi and the other gypsies would think it wrong as none of them would ever marry a Gorgio, which was the gypsy word for a non-gypsy.

It was so wonderful, so utterly unbelievable!

And as she had said herself – perfect.

She felt the tears come into her eyes.

How could any man prove his love more vividly and more determinedly?

'Thank you – God – thank you,' whispered Della and she felt as she prayed that her father and mother were smiling at her.

It took her a little while to undress as the Marquis had told her to do and to find a nightgown in her bag.

She was exhausted even though she was wildly elated.

She felt she had experienced a miracle beyond all miracles!

She slipped into bed and only as her head touched the pillow did she think, for the first time, about Jason.

Now she realised she need no longer be afraid as the Marquis would be there to protect her.

If she was married to him, no one, not even the Duke, could hurt her.

'I love him – I adore him,' she murmured to herself.

She felt, as she fell asleep, that he was like an Archangel from Heaven protecting her from her enemies.

She was no longer afraid.

*

Della must have slept for a very long time.

She only awoke because she heard someone moving about the room.

For a moment she could not think who it could be or where she was.

Then she remembered how the Marquis had brought her here and had told her she was to go to sleep.

For a moment she was afraid to open her eyes.

Perhaps now it was all not true – an incredibly improbable dream or just a figment of her imagination.

Yet the bed did not seem like the small bed she had occupied in Mireli's caravan.

She opened her eyes to find the sun was shining through the windows into a large and beautifully furnished bedroom.

Della felt a little tremor run through her body. If this

was where she was, then it *was* true that the Marquis wanted to marry her.

She would be his wife.

Someone came to the bedside and she looked up to see an elderly woman.

"Are you awake, miss?" she asked. "I'm his Lordship's Nanny and he's told me to look after you and to get you ready for your wedding."

Della drew in her breath.

"Wedding!" she murmured.

"It's the best day of my life," exclaimed Nanny. "I've been praying his Lordship'll find himself a wife and when he told me the good news I've never seen him so happy."

Before Della could answer she said in a different tone of voice,

"I've brought you something to eat, miss, because you've missed breakfast, luncheon and tea."

"What is the time?"

"It's getting on for six o'clock," Nanny told her, "and I thinks when you've eaten what I've brought you, you'd like a bath."

"I would indeed," agreed Della enthusiastically.

It had not been possible to have a bath while she was staying with the gypsies and it had been very difficult to wash in just a small bowl.

She sat up in bed and Nanny brought her a tray with a large mug of soup.

Excited though she was, Della felt hungry and when she had finished the soup there was a dish of fresh trout, which she suspected came from the lake. It was cooked with a cream sauce and she enjoyed every mouthful.

Nanny poured her out a glass of champagne to drink with it.

After the fish there was a light soufflé followed by a variety of fruit.

Della felt Nanny would be disappointed if she did not eat everything she was offered and she only made a protest when she was given a second helping of fruit.

She enjoyed a cup of coffee after she had finished the meal.

Nanny had not talked to her while she was eating and now she carried away the tray.

Two housemaids brought in a round bath and set it down on the mat in front of the fireplace. There were two large brass cans to follow it and Della knew that one contained hot water and the other cold.

The maids disappeared and she climbed out bed and into the bath. The water was scented with what she recognised as the perfume of white violets.

When she finished washing herself Nanny helped to dry her in a large Turkish towel.

It was then, for the first time, she wondered what she should wear if she was indeed to be married as the Marquis had insisted.

She guessed the service would be in his private Chapel as it was obvious a large house like Clare Court would have one.

At the same time she worried that she would not look as pretty as she would like to be for she only had the rather plain gowns she had brought with her.

Nanny went to the wardrobe.

"There are two wedding dresses for you to choose

from," she announced grandly, "and I thinks, as I've measured them against one of your own, they'll fit you almost as if they've been made for you."

"*Wedding dresses!*" cried Della. "How could you have wedding dresses here?"

Nanny gave a little laugh.

"Very easily. Every bride in the last two hundred years has left their wedding dresses in what we calls the Museum."

"I have not seen it."

"His Lordship'll show it to you, but it's in the East wing. Most visitors prefer to see the pictures in the gallery on the other side of the house."

"You have a collection of wedding dresses!" sighed Della, as if to herself. She could hardly believe it.

Nanny lifted down two lovely gowns from the wardrobe.

"This one was worn by his Lordship's mother," explained Nanny, "and the other by his grandmother."

They were both classic in shape and made, Della knew, by the master hands of a great designer.

One was of rather heavy satin and the other was of chiffon which reminded Della of the gowns worn by the Greek Goddesses.

She thought instinctively that was how the Marquis would like her to look.

When Nanny put it on her she found it fitted her perfectly and in fact gave her an almost classical look as if she had just stepped out of the Acropolis in Athens.

"That's the one I hoped you'd choose," crowed Nanny with satisfaction. "Now I have the veil which is worn by all the Clare brides. It is, I've been told, over three hundred years old."

`The veil was made of exquisite lace and after Nanny had arranged Della's hair she placed the veil over her head. It fell down on each side of her face, but did not cover it.

It was then that Nanny opened a leather box which was standing on the dressing table and in it was the most beautiful tiara Della had ever seen, made of diamonds in the shape of flowers.

It made her think not only of the formal flowers in the garden, but the wild flowers that grew in the woods. She thought when the Marquis was choosing it for her the same idea was in his mind too.

Only *he* could be so understanding and know exactly what she wanted without her putting it into words.

When she looked at herself in the mirror, she thought once again that she must be dreaming.

This is how she had always wanted to look for the man she loved and she thought it could never happen because she would not be lucky enough to find him.

She had taken some time in bathing and dressing and now Della realised it was nearly seven o'clock. She looked at Nanny enquiringly who told her,

"Your wedding's to take place on the hour and his Lordship'll not want you to be late."

"I think I am to be married in the Chapel," said Della. "But how can it be legal when the banns have not been read. I cannot believe that his Lordship has a Special Licence."

Nanny gave a little laugh.

"It's something I would've asked myself if I didn't live here. There are still private Chapels which are allowed to marry anyone without the formalities the people expect elsewhere."

"Of course! I remember now," exclaimed Della, "and his Lordship's Chapel is one of them."

"It's because Clare Court has been here for so long," said Nanny proudly. "It were built originally when Queen Elizabeth was on the throne."

She spoke with a pride which Della felt was rather touching. She knew in the future that was what she would feel herself.

Even as she thought of it, everything seemed too incredible to be true.

"Now come along," urged Nanny, "I'll take you down to the Chapel. His Lordship has left a bouquet of flowers for you."

She opened the door as she spoke.

She brought in a beautiful bouquet made up of white orchids with just a touch of pink in the centre.

As she took the flowers in her hands Nanny said,

"Be kind to my baby, I've loved him as if he were my own ever since he were born. I'd give my life to make him happy."

"I promise you, Nanny, I will do my very best to make him the happiest man in the world," answered Della. "And thank you so very much for helping me."

She bent to kiss the old woman's cheeks and saw the tears in her eyes.

Then walking slowly because her veil trailed a little behind her, she let Nanny guide her along the corridor.

They did not use the impressive staircase that came up from the hall and Della guessed that there would be a special staircase leading from the Master Suite down to the Chapel. It would be a unique feature the Adam brothers would have designed for Clare Court and many other great houses.

When they duly arrived at the first step, Nanny beckoned her to descend first.

As she walked slowly down the Adam staircase, Della could hear an organ playing very softly in the distance.

Then as she reached the ground floor, she saw an impressive gothic door immediately in front of her.

Opening the door hesitatingly, she found that the Marquis was waiting for her. Two more steps and she was at his side.

He was looking at her with an expression of love and devotion in his eyes.

She felt as if the stars were shining above her head and the light of the moon enveloped them both.

There was no need for words and the Marquis held out his arm and she slipped her hand into it.

As she did so she was aware that he was wearing his decorations and they glittered in the light of the candles on the altar.

The Chapel was small but very beautiful and behind the cross on the altar the sun was streaming through an exquisite stained glass window.

It seemed to Della as if there was light everywhere.

A light that was Divine and Heavenly.

The Marquis drew her a few steps up the aisle and a Priest was waiting for them at the altar.

When the organ lapsed into silence he started the marriage service.

Della felt as if every instinct in her body and her heart were extended towards the Marquis and she knew he felt the same.

When he placed the ring carefully on her finger they were already joined together by every breath they drew. Their hearts and souls were linked irrevocably and could never be divided.

They knelt in front of the Priest and he blessed them and Della was sure that her father and mother were blessing her too.

God had answered her prayers.

He enveloped them both with a wonder and a glory they could never lose.

When they rose to their feet the Priest knelt down in front of the altar and the Marquis holding Della by the hand drew her out of the Chapel.

The only witness who had been present at their marriage was Nanny and she was wiping the tears from her eyes as the Marquis took Della away from the Chapel.

They walked up the staircase she had descended with Nanny and he opened a door on the landing. Della thought it must be the entrance to the Master Suite and she was not mistaken.

It was a lovely room with sky blue carpet and curtains and a huge canopied bed with gold cupids occupied the centre of the room.

For a moment Della could only see flowers. The whole room had been decorated with endless blooms and they were all white.

Never had she seen such a profusion of lilies, orchids and roses which scented the air with their sublime fragrance, making the room seem to Della an essential part of the enchanted world into which the Marquis had spirited her.

He was looking at the surprise and excitement in her eyes.

"You are *so* lovely," he sighed in a deep voice. "I am still afraid you are not real, my adorable Della, and you might vanish in a puff of smoke."

"Nothing that has happened since you came to the gypsy camp has seemed real," replied Della, "but as you said, it is all so marvellous and so perfect that I think we must both have died and are in Heaven."

"You have not died, my precious one," the Marquis assured her. "Now I am able to tell you how much I love you and how much you mean to me."

His voice had deepened as he continued,

"But first I am going to take off my finery and you, my lovely bride, must do the same."

As he spoke he lifted her veil and started to undo the back of her wedding gown.

For a moment he paused.

She thought he was going to pull her into his arms and kiss her. Instead, almost as if he ordered himself to obey his own instructions, he left the room.

He disappeared through what Della imagined was a communicating door into his dressing room.

'How can he be so wonderful and at the same time so well organised?' she asked herself.

But she knew he was right. If he wanted to kiss her it would be tiresome to have her wreath, her veil and her gown in the way.

She placed the veil on the dressing table and it was easy to slip out of her Greek wedding gown.

She was not surprised to see one of her prettiest nightgowns lying on the bed.

She took the pins out of her hair and her long golden tresses fell over her shoulders.

She lay back against the lace-edged pillows and waited breathlessly.

The evening sun was shining through the windows and its rays seemed to glitter on everything they touched and even the flowers looked more exquisite than they could ever have seemed.

'Only a fairy Princess,' Della told herself, 'could be blessed with such a wonderful setting and I am afraid it might vanish before my husband sees it.'

She blushed as she referred to the Marquis as her husband.

It all seemed so extraordinary.

How could she ever have guessed when she first met him that he was the man of her dreams? The man she thought she would never find because he did not really exist.

The door opened and the Marquis entered and stood for a moment looking at the room.

Then he turned his gaze at Della waiting for him in the large bed with its golden cupids over her head.

As he moved nearer to her she realised he was staring at her hair.

"That is how I have always wanted you to look," he breathed, "but how is it possible?"

Della smiled.

"It is quite simple. I am not, as you supposed, a gypsy."

The Marquis sat down on the edge of the bed facing her.

"Not a gypsy!" he exclaimed. "Then why were you with them? How can you tell fortunes so brilliantly and if I have not married a gypsy, then *who* are you?"

Della gave a little laugh.

"It is a long story – but – "

It was not possible to say any more.

The Marquis had put his arms round her and was kissing her fervently.

At first his kisses were gentle as if she was so precious that he was afraid of hurting her. Then he became more possessive as if he wanted to make sure she was his and could not escape from him.

Somehow Della was never quite certain when it happened, but they became closer still.

His kisses were so passionate and demanding it was impossible to think, only to feel.

Not only her whole body became part of him, but her heart and her soul were his as well.

They belonged completely to each other.

When the Marquis carried her up to the sky on the wings of ecstasy, they were no longer two people but one.

*

A long time later the Marquis murmured,

"My darling, my precious, how can I ever have guessed that anyone could be as perfect as you? Or I would find you of all unexpected places in a gypsy caravan?"

Della chuckled.

"And how could I find the man of my dreams in the

same place? In addition he is the star I always believed would be somewhere in the world and he would love me as I love him?"

"You do love me?" the Marquis demanded in a deep voice.

"I love you – and adore you, my husband. Promise me you will never love anyone else because if you do I shall only – want to die."

"I have never loved anyone as I love you, my darling, and I know it would be impossible for me to think about let alone marry anyone else. As you have just said we have been looking for each other for perhaps a million years. Now we are together and that is how I am convinced we shall remain for all eternity."

He spoke from the depths of his heart and Della gave a cry of sheer happiness.

"This is just what I believe and I love you and love you, until it is – *impossible* for me to say it in – any other – words."

The Marquis did not ask her to try and instead he kissed her again and again until they were both breathless.

Then as her head rested on his shoulder and he kissed her golden hair, he said,

"We are going away first thing tomorrow morning on our honeymoon. My new yacht is waiting for us at Southampton so we do not have very far to go."

It was then Della remembered something.

To reach Southampton they would almost pass her own home and her uncle must be told what had happened to her. Yet she had no wish for the present to even think what the consequences of her news might be.

"Now you are worried," the Marquis interrupted her

thoughts, "and that is something I cannot allow you to be."

Della thought quickly.

"Let us leave all the explanations about ourselves until tomorrow," she suggested. "Tonight is so blissful in this enchanted room, I only want to think of you and love."

"It is completely impossible for me to think of anything but you," he answered. "You are quite right, my precious Della, you are mine and no one can take you away from me. We will leave all the explanations until later."

"I knew you would understand as you have always understood from the very first moment I met you."

"I still do not believe you are real, my Della. Promise you will not suddenly vanish with the Gods to Olympus or into the pool in the woods where all I can see will be your reflection in the water."

"I will do – nothing of the sort," Della promised. "I am so wildly – happy to be – close to you like this, the world outside is of no importance."

"And it will never be," agreed the Marquis firmly.

It was almost as if he was making a vow.

Della sensed that he was thinking of how angry and shocked his family would be if he had married someone of no consequence.

The truth was very different, but still she did not wish to talk about it tonight.

To mention Jason and the Duke might spoil the exquisite wonder of their wedding night and she did not want him to think of anything or anyone but her and she wanted to blot out the memory of the fear that had made her run away.

Moving even closer she put her arms round the Marquis's neck and drew his lips down to hers.

Then he was kissing her again.

His hand was touching her body and their hearts were beating frantically against each other.

This was the wild unfettered music of the woods.

The water was falling from the fountain.

The glitter of the stars was coming out in the sky overhead.

This was the perfection of love.

The love which would never die and which was theirs for ever.

*

The following morning, although they had not slept for very long, the Marquis insisted on having breakfast early.

When they walked outside Della saw the carriage which was to take them to Southampton. It was drawn by a team of perfectly matched chestnuts.

The 'travelling chariot', as it was named, was very light and beside the driver's seat there was only one small place for the groom behind the hood.

The horses were finer than any team Della had ever seen and the Marquis smiled at her enthusiasm as she patted them.

Their luggage had already left, before they came down to breakfast.

"Nanny says she has packed everything she thought you would need," the Marquis informed Della, "but I dare say you can collect a few dresses if we stop at your home as you have asked me to do."

"Yes, of course," she agreed.

She had told him they would be passing very near to her home on their way to Southampton and she wanted to introduce him to the relative who had brought her up.

"My father and mother are dead," she explained, "and I must tell my uncle what has happened to me."

"Yes, of course, my darling."

The Marquis had readily concurred with her request, but he had, however, spoken indifferently and Della suspected that he resented this intrusion of reality back into their lives.

When they left Clare Court he drove the horses rapidly with an expertise which Della expected from him. He was looking so happy that he seemed almost to vibrate a burning light towards her.

As the servants said goodbye and waved as they drove down the drive Della knew they were delighted at how happy their Master was.

They reached her uncle's village at about twelve o'clock, rather earlier than Della had expected, but the Marquis had given his team their heads. He was an exceptional driver and Della felt sure he would break every record on the roads.

She thought now that on reaching her home they might stay for luncheon.

She was, however, not quite sure if that would be what her husband would desire and she was feeling nervous.

What would her uncle say to her marriage without his permission or even an invitation to the wedding?

The Marquis turned his horses in at the gate and Della was conscious of an expression of surprise in his eyes when he saw the house.

The pink Elizabethan bricks looked most attractive in the sunshine and Della was certain that he had not expected anything so beautiful or so ancient.

He drew up the horses outside the front door.

Storton came running down the steps to greet the carriage.

"It's good to see you, Miss Della!" he exclaimed. "His Lordship's been worrying as to what had happened to you."

"I am quite safe, Storton," Della assured him. "Is his Lordship in the study?"

"Writing away, Miss Della, as might be expected."

Della walked in through the front door and as the Marquis joined her, she said,

"Come and meet my uncle. I am a little frightened in case he is angry with me for getting married without his permission."

"Leave everything to me," replied the Marquis. "You know, my precious, I will not have you upset for anything."

Della did not reply. She just walked to the study door and opened it.

Her uncle looked up, saw her and gave out an exclamation of delight.

"Della, you're back!"

She ran towards him.

"Please forgive me, Uncle Edward, for running away and for being married without telling you about it."

Lord Lainden stared at her in astonishment.

"*Married!*"

"I have brought my husband here to meet you," added Della breathlessly.

The two men looked at each other.

Then Lord Lainden spoke slowly,

"Perhaps I am mistaken but surely you are Kelvin Chorlton."

"And you are Lord Lainden," replied the Marquis. "I enjoyed your speech in the House of Lords last month and agreed with every word."

Lord Lainden held out his hand.

"I was exceedingly fond of your father," he said looking confused, "but I cannot quite understand what Della has just said and why you are here."

The Marquis smiled.

"We were married yesterday. It was a case of love at first sight and I was terrified of losing her."

"Married!" cried Lord Lainden again. "I find it difficult to believe – "

Della held on to his arm.

"We are so happy, Uncle Edward. And if the Duke is disagreeable then I am sure Kelvin can find you a house on his vast estate."

"Which Duke is that?" asked the Marquis, "and why should he be disagreeable?"

"The reason – I ran away – to the gypsies – "

"So Della, you were with the gypsies!" her uncle ejaculated. "I wondered where on earth you could have gone, but it never struck me you would go with Piramus and Lendi. But I am sure they looked after you well."

"They dyed my hair to disguise me as a gypsy and Kelvin has been brave enough to marry me believing I was one of them," Della told him simply.

She slipped her hand into the Marquis's as she spoke, half afraid he would be annoyed at her deception.

But he only said,

"How could you have deceived me so cleverly and how could you have told fortunes so well, if not better, than Lendi?"

"It is my Scottish blood which makes me capable of reading peoples' minds," answered Della. "And I had to escape form the Earl of Rannock."

The Marquis stared at her incredulously.

"Rannock!" he repeated sharply. "What have you got to do with that young swine?"

Della looked at her uncle.

"His father, the Duke, was determined that I should marry him. That is why I ran away."

The Marquis put his arm round her protectively

"Thank God you did so," he sighed. "I would not want my worst enemy to have anything at all to do with Rannock!"

"The Duke was determined I should save him from – himself," Della stammered. "And, because I was frightened he might make life very uncomfortable for Uncle Edward, I ran away to try and work out a solution to the dilemma."

She smiled before she added softly,

"And – I – found – *you*."

"For which I thank God, the stars, the moon and everyone else who might have been involved!"

He looked at Lord Lainden before he asked,

"Are you really likely to have any trouble with

Marchwood over this?"

"I thought for one moment that we might be in a great deal of trouble," explained Lord Lainden. "But as it happened, the most amazing thing has occurred."

"What is it?" asked Della breathlessly.

"The rakish Earl has fallen in love," replied her uncle.

Della stared at him.

"Not with – me," she faltered.

"No, my dear, you are quite safe. As soon as you disappeared he spent every day, as far as I can ascertain, with Lady Southgate. She is taking as much trouble over him as she is taking over her puppies. And believe it or not he looks like becoming a reformed character thanks to her."

"Are you saying she will marry him?"

"Actually the village knows far more about the affair than I do," answered Lord Lainden. "But that is exactly what she is considering she might do."

Della clasped her hands together.

"Oh, Uncle Edward, how wonderful! This means the Duke will not be unpleasant to you and you will still be able to ride his horses."

"I think," the Marquis intervened, "it would be much more sensible if your uncle took a look at my Dower House which is empty at the moment. It is not unlike this house and it would give me great pleasure to have someone so distinguished living on my estate. I feel sure like you, my darling, that Lord Lainden will enjoy the use of my library."

"What a really glorious idea," enthused Della. "Oh, please, Uncle Edward, do consider it. I would love you to be near us and when Kelvin can spare me I can go on helping you with your book."

"It is certainly something I would like to consider," he responded. "And thank you, Kelvin, for such a generous offer."

"I think actually I am being quite selfish," added the Marquis. "I do not wish Della to be out of my sight for one moment, and it will be far better for her to run down to the Dower House than to tell me she has to come here to see you in case you are lonely."

The two men laughed and Della pleaded,

"Please, Uncle Edward, be ready to move in as soon as we return from our honeymoon."

They talked about the proposed move over luncheon and when they drove off the Marquis said,

"My precious, how could anything be so perfect? My family will be ecstatic with joy that I have married someone not only as beautiful as you, but who is the niece of your uncle whom they all respect."

"I shall never forget that you wanted to marry me when you thought I was only a gypsy!"

Della moved a little nearer to him as she spoke and her hand was on his knee.

The Marquis took his eyes off the road to look down at her.

"You look so incredibly beautiful and if you speak to me with that little catch in your voice which I find irresistible, I shall forget I am driving and we shall have an accident."

Della laughed.

"You are too good a driver for that. At the same time I want you to tell me that you like my hair the colour it is and that you are glad you did not have to fight for me because your relations thought you had picked me up in the gutter."

"No one who ever looked at you could think such a travesty of the truth," answered the Marquis. "Equally I admit it makes my life very much easier than I expected. But nothing in the world would have prevented me from marrying you anyway. You have stolen my heart and I would always have been crippled by the loss of it if I had not married you."

"Oh, darling, darling Kelvin, I love you so. It is not only the exciting compliments you pay me or the fact that when you kiss me you carry me up to Heaven. It is also because you are so kind, so clever and so understanding."

"I adore and worship you," sighed the Marquis. "And the sooner we sail away, the better. I want to tell you just how much you mean to me and it is far easer to say so without words."

Della gave a little laugh of sheer happiness.

Then as she looked ahead she could see the outskirts of Southampton in the far distance.

The Marquis's yacht was waiting for them.

They would set off on a voyage of discovery which would make them inseparable because they were both longing for the joy and bliss of their divine future together.

It was a treasure beyond price.

It was the ecstasy and wonder which God has given to man.

Quite simply it is *love*.

The Love which comes from God, and makes those who are fortunate enough to find it, a part of God in this life and forever.